PHALANXES OF ATLANS

PHALANXES OF ATLANS

F. VAN WYCK MASON

PULP CLASSICS

PHALANXES OF ATLANS

Originally published as a two-part serial in
Astounding Stories, February-March 1931.

Pulp Classics is published by Wildside Press, LLC
www.wildsidebooks.com

PHALANXES OF ATLANS

CHAPTER I

The ice suddenly gave way under his foot, hurling Victor Nelson violently forward to lie in the deep snow at the bottom of a tiny crevasse, down which the merciless gale moaned like an anguished demon.

"It's no use," he muttered bitterly. "We've fought hard, but we're done for."

He lay still, stupidly watching his breath form tiny beads of ice on the ends of the fur which lined his parka. Until that moment he had not realized how thoroughly exhausted he was. Every muscle of his starved, bruised body ached unbearably. It wasn't so bad lying there in the soft snow. He could rest, then look later for the ice hummock behind which the plane lay sheltered. Rest! That's what he needed, a good long rest.

But deep within him, a primal instinct stabbed his waning consciousness. "No," he gasped, and blinked his reddened eyes behind smoked goggles which dulled the shimmer of the aurora. "If I stop, I'll never get up."

Shaken by the terrific velocity of the arctic gale he numbly clambered to his feet, then stooped with a stiff awkward motion to retrieve a Winchester rifle which lay half buried in the snow beside the blurred imprint of his body.

"Wonder if Alden had any better luck?" The question burned dully in his brain. "Don't suppose so; there can't be anything alive in this God-awful wilderness." As he stumbled on he found no answer in an unbroken vista of wind-scored ice and drifting snow that, swirling high into the air, momentarily cut off the view of that black line of ice-capped mountains barely visible on the horizon.

"Yes, if he hasn't found anything, we'll be dead or frozen stiff before tomorrow."

His soul—that of a true explorer—revolted, not at the thought of death, but that his and Alden's courageously won discovery of a majestic mountain range towering high over a polar region marked "unexplored" on the maps would now never be made public.

Leaning forward against the merciless icy blast he painfully picked his way over a treacherous ice ridge, to be faintly encouraged by the fact that the towerlike hummock of ice marking the position of the plane now lay but a few hundred yards ahead.

Bitterly he cursed that demon of ill-fortune who had sent the blinding snow storm which had forced down the plane ten long days ago at the very beginning of its triumphant return flight to the base at Cape Richards. Since that hour the storm gods had emptied the vials of their wrath upon the luckless explorers. Day after day, cyclonic winds made all thought of a take-off suicidal in the extreme. Three days ago the last of their food had given out, and, he mused, starvation is an ill companion for despair.

Slip, slide and fall! On he fought until the final barrier was reached and he stood staring hopelessly down into a small natural amphitheater which sheltered the great monoplane. The ship was still there, its engine snugged in a canvas shroud and with the soft, dry snow banked up high in the lee of its silver gray fuselage. Numbly, like a man in the grip of a painful coma, Nelson shielded his face with a furry hand to scan the surrounding terrain. "Hell!" The door block of the igloo they had built was still snowed up; Alden was not there!

"He's not back," he muttered, while his body swayed beneath the gale which smote him with fierce, unseen fists.

"Poor devil, I hope he hasn't lost the way."

All the bitterness of undeserved defeat stung his soul as he started down the incline into the hollow.

Suddenly he paused. The rifle flew into the ready position and his chilled thumb drew back the hammer. "What's this?" On the snow at his feet was a bright, scarlet splash, dreadfully distinct against the white background. While his dazed brain struggled to register what his eyes saw, he looked to the right and left and discovered several more of the hideous spots. Then an object that gleamed dully in the polar twilight attracted his attention. He lumbered forward, stooped stiffly and caught up a long, half round strip of bronze.

"What? Why? Oh—I'm crazy. I'm seeing things!" The pain in his empty stomach was now becoming excruciating. To steady himself he shut his eyes, shook his head as though to clear it, then looked again at that strip of metal in his hand. Attached to it were two slender strips of leather like straps, ending in small, bronze buckles.

"Why, it's not from the plane," he stammered aloud. "Damned if it doesn't look like a greave the old Greek warriors used to wear to protect their shins."

Suddenly alarmed and mystified beyond words, he shuffled forward over the snow, the greave yet clutched in a fur gloved hand. Presently two more objects, already half buried by the stinging, swirling drifts, caught his attention. One was the stock of Alden's rifle, protruding starkly brown from the unrelieved whiteness, and the other was a broken wooden shaft that ended a graceful but wickedly sharp bronze spear head.

"I've either gone crazy," he said, "or I'm delirious. Yes, I must be clean nutty! There *couldn't* be a human settlement within a thousand miles. Let's see what's happened."

* * * * *

In the snow of a little wind-sheltered space behind the igloo he discovered the unmistakable and ominous signs of a struggle. An indefinite number of footprints, blurred but enormous in size, were marked in the snow. Here and there deep furrows mutely testified how Alden and the enemies against whom he struggled had reeled back and forth in vicious combat over a considerable area. Then, shaken by a new fear, he discovered Alden's left glove and a rag of some peculiar thick material that seemed to have a metallic finish. But what aroused his gravest fears were the numerous splashes of blood that here and there streaked the snow in gruesome relief.

Only a moment Nelson stood, shaken by the merciless wind, scanning the piece of bronzed armor between his gloved hands with a fresh interest. It was beautifully fashioned, and decorated at the knee point with the wonderfully wrought figure of a dolphin.

If he could only think clearly! But his brain seemed to lie in a red-hot skull. "Whatever's happened," he muttered, "I'd better not waste time; they couldn't have been here so long ago. Poor Alden! I wonder what kind of devils caught him?"

Even before he had finished the sentence the aviator had taken up the partially obliterated trail of spattered blood drops. That what he sought appeared to be a marauding party of giants restrained him not at all. The one clear thought burning in his weary brain was that Richard Alden, his best friend—the man with whom he had traveled over half the world, by whose side he had faced many a perilous situation—must at that moment lie in peril, the extent of which he could only surmise.

"Must have been about a dozen of them," he said thickly. And, holding the Winchester ready, he commenced once more to plod on through the stinging sheets of wind-driven ice particles. More than once he had great difficulty in not losing that crimson trail, for here and there the restless, white crystals completely blotted out the splashes.

All at once Nelson checked his pathetically slow progress, finding himself on the top of an eminence, looking down in what appeared to be a vastly deep natural amphitheater of snow and ice. At the bottom, and perhaps a hundred yards distant, was a curious black oval from which appeared to rise a dense, wind-whipped column of whitish vapor.

"My eyes must be going back on me," muttered Nelson through stiffened lips. How intolerably heavy his fur suit seemed! His strength was about gone and that curious black mouthlike circle seemed infinitely far away. But, spurred by fears for his friend, he started downward for the precipitious trail leading directly towards it.

Once he stepped inside the crater, he became conscious of a terrific side pressure which gripped him as a whirlpool seizes a luckless swimmer. The wind buffetted him from all angles, dealing him powerful blows on face and body, which, too strong for his weary body, sent him reeling weakly, drunkenly across the hard, glare ice towards the vortex. Twice he slipped, each time finding it harder to arise. But at last he approached what on closer inspection proved to be a subterranean vent of black rock.

"Steam!" he gasped. "It's steam coming out of there!"

Swayed by a dozen conflicting emotions, he paused, the Winchester barrel wavering like a reed in his enfeebled grasp.

"The whole thing's crazy," he decided. "I must be frozen

and lying somewhere, delirious. Poor Dick! Can't help him much now."

Like a man in a nightmare who advances but feels nothing under his feet, Nelson staggered on towards that huge, gaping aperture of black rock. On the threshold a pool of melted snow water made him stare.

"Hell!" he said. "It's only a volcanic vent of some kind." Then dimly came the recollection of Eskimo legends concerning thermal springs beyond the desolate and unknown reaches of Grant Land.

His mind in an indescribable turmoil, Nelson splashed across a hundred yards of sodden snow, then shivered on wading knee deep through a pool of melted ice. Now he stood on the very threshold of that awful opening, dense clouds of vapor beating warmly against his chilled features.

His goggles fogged at once, blinding him effectively as, with reason staggering under the accumulated stress of starvation and the circumstances of Alden's disappearance, he groped his way a few feet into the vent. With his left hand he pulled up the glasses from his sunken, blood-shot eyes.

"It's warm, by God!" he cried in astonishment as the skin exposed by lifting the goggles came in contact with the air. "Must be some kind of earth-warmed cave."

Increasingly mystified, he caught up his rifle and strode on down the passage, at that moment illuminated by the last unearthly rays of the aurora borealis. A single, dazzling beam played before him like a powerful search-light, to light a high vaulted tunnel of basalt rocks which were distorted by some long-gone convulsion of the earth into a hundred weird cleavages and faults. For that brief instant he found he could see perhaps a hundred feet down into a high roofed passage, along the top of which poured a tremendous stream of billowing, writhing steam.

"If this doesn't beat all," he murmured; but for all of his apprehension he did not pause. Those bloody splashes bespeaking Alden's pressing need urged him on. "Looks like I'm taking a one way trip into Hell itself. Well, we'll soon see."

Slipping and sliding over an almost impassable array of black rocks and boulders, Nelson fought his way forward, conscious that with every stride the air grew damper and warmer. Soon trickles of sweat were pouring down over his chest, tickling unbearably.

Then all at once the ray of light faded, leaving him immersed in a blackness equalled only by the gloom of a subterranean vault. He stopped and, resting his rifle against a nearby invisible rock, threw back the parka hood and pulled off his gloves. He was amazed to feel how warm the strong air current was on his hands.

"Beats all," he muttered heavily. "I wonder where they've taken Alden?"

Meanwhile his hands groped through fur garments now wet with melted-snow and ice particles, searching for the catch to open that pocket in which lay a small but powerful electric flashlight, an instrument without which no far-flying aviator finds himself. After a moment's fumbling, his yet stiffened fingers encountered the cylindrical flash and, with a low cry of satisfaction, he drew it forth to press the button.

"Mighty useful. I—" The words stopped, frozen on his lips. Before the parka edge his close cropped hair seemed to rise, and his breath stopped midway in his lungs. Sharp electric shocks shook him, for there, half revealed in the feeble flashlight's glare, was a sight which shook his sanity to the snapping point. Not fifty feet away two eyes, large as dinner plates, with narrow vertical red irises, were trained on him. Rooted to the ground by the paralysis of utter horror, Nelson saw that their color was a weird, unhealthy, greenish white, rather like the color of a radio-light watch dial.

Strangely intense, these huge orbs wavered not at all, filling him with an unnameable dread, while the strong odor of musk assailed his nostrils. The flashlight slipped from between Nelson's fingers and, no longer having his thumb on the button, flickered out.

Helpless, Nelson stood transfixed against a boulder, aware that the strange, musky scent was becoming stronger. Then to his ears came a dry scrabbling as of some large body stealthily advancing. Those horrible, unearthly eyes were coming nearer! Fierce, terrible shocks of fear gripped the exhausted aviator. Then the impulse of self-preservation, that most elementary of all instincts, forced him to snatch up the rifle, to sight hastily, blindly, between those two, great greenish eyes. Choking out a strangled sob of desperation, Nelson made his trembling finger close over the cold strip of steel that must be the trigger.

Like a stage trick, the cavern was momentarily lit by a strong, orange yellow glare. Then the Winchester's report thundered and roared deafeningly; coincidentally arose a nerve-shattering scream. An exhalation, foul as a corpse long unburied, fanned his face. Terrified, he flattened to the rock wall as a huge, though dangerously agile body hurtled by with the speed of a runaway horse. Presently followed the sound of a ponderous fall, then a series of shrill, ear-piercing gibberings and squeakings, like those of a titanic rat—squeaks that rang like the chorus of Hell itself. Gradually they grew fainter, while in the darkness the heavy air of the tunnel became rank with the odor of clotting blood.

Nelson remained where he was, shaking like a frightened horse and bathed with a cold sweat.

"Wonder what it was?" he muttered numbly.

He broke off, for in the terrible darkness sounded a low but perfectly audible *thud! thud! thud! thud!*—and also the subtle noise of some rough surface rasping gently over the stone. His nerves crisped and shrieked for relief.

"It's coming again!" he told himself, and ejected the spent cartridge from the Winchester. "No use—it'll get me, but I may as well fight as long as I can."

Even stronger grew the musty smell of blood while that uncanny *thud! thud!* sound continued at regular intervals. Nelson waited, breath halted and finger on trigger, but still the darkness yielded no glimpse of those awful saucer-like eyes.

Emboldened, he stooped and, jerking off his left glove, commenced to grope among the boulders. Somewhere near at his feet the flashlight must be lying. Hoping against hope that its fall had not shattered the bulb, he ran his fingers over the cold, damp stones, every instant expecting to feel the clutch of the unseen monster. How tiny, how puny he was! All at once his fingers encountered the smooth familiar shape of the flash and he raised it cautiously through the darkness. Patiently he shifted the Winchester to his left hand in order to set the flashlight on the top of a flat rock, pointing it as nearly as he could determine in the direction from whence came those ominous, stealthy sounds.

"Guess I'll switch on the light," he decided, "and trust to drop whatever it is before it reaches me."

Taking a fresh grip on his quivering nerves, Nelson

cautiously cocked the .38-55, cuddled the familiar stock to his shoulder. He sighted, then with his right hand pushed down the catch lever of the flashlight.

Instantly a dazzling white beam shot forth to shatter the gloom. The hair on the back of Nelson's hands itched unbearably, while the cold fingers of madness clutched at his brain, for the sight which met his eyes all but bereft him of his wavering sanity. There, belly up, across a low ridge of basalt, lay a hideous reptile, which in form faintly resembled an enormous and fantastic kangaroo. Its scabby belly was of the unhealthy yellow of a grub, a hue which gave way to a leaden gray as the wart-covered skin reached the back. Two enormous hind legs, each thick as a man's torso and each equipped with three dagger-like talons, struck out in helpless fury at the air, while a long, lizard-like tail threshed powerfully back and forth, scattering ponderous boulders right and left as though they had been marbles. The flashlight being trained as it was, the monster's head and forequarters were invisible, all save two very much smaller and shorter front legs which, like the hinder ones, clawed spasmodically.

"The D. T's!" gasped Nelson, conscious that he was trembling like an aspen. He suppressed a wild desire to laugh. "Yes, I've gone crazy!"

He glanced downwards and leaped swiftly back, for, creeping over the stones towards his fur outer boots, meandered a wide rivulet of bright scarlet blood. From its surface rose small curling feathers of steam which, drifting towards the tunnel's roof, merged with that gray, vaporous current flowing steadily towards the sunless Arctic expanse outside.

It took Nelson a long five minutes to sufficiently recover his equilibrium for action. All he could do was to stare at that grotesque, gargoyle-like creature as it writhed in leisurely and persistent death throes.

"Guess I winged it all right! My God, what a nasty beast! Looks like one of those allosaurs I read about in college. It couldn't be, though—that tribe of dinosaurs died out five million years ago."

Cautiously he scrambled around among the high black stones, casting the search light beams before him and holding the Winchester always ready in his hand while trying to recall snatches of palaeontology studied at college long years ago.

"Yes, it must be a survival of one of the carnivorous dinosaurs," he decided, then paused, increasingly conscious of that steady thudding noise. What caused it?

At last he found himself before the creature's gigantic and repulsive head which lay limp over a blood bathed stone, huge jaws partially open, and serrated rows of wicked, stiletto-sharp teeth gleaming yellowly in the flashlight's rays. The head in shape was bullet-like, ending in a blunt nose as big as a bushel basket and in two prominent nostrils. The green, lidless eyes were still open, shining faintly, and seemed to follow his movements, but the steaming blood poured with the force of a small hose from between triple row of bayonetlike teeth that curved inward like those of a shark, to splash and bubble freely to the rock floor and to dribble horribly over the warty, gray hide.

Then Nelson discovered an amazing fact. About the great scaly neck, thick as a boy's waist, was fastened a ponderous collar, set with short, sharp spikes.

Nelson gasped. "What in hell!" he cried. "This damn thing's somebody's property!" His mind, staggered at the thought of dealing with a race that could and would domesticate such a hideous monster. "Well, it's no use standing here," he muttered, wiping the sweat from his eyes. "This isn't getting poor Alden away from those devils."

Thud! thud! In the act of turning he paused, listened once more. Then he discovered to his amazement that the heart of the apparently dead reptile was still beating strongly. He could even see the yellow skin of its belly rise and fall. The effect was grotesque, uncanny.

"Of course," muttered the shaken aviator, "I'd forgotten a reptile's ganglions will keep on beating for hours, like that shark we killed off Paumotu. Its heart didn't stop for five hours."

Leaving the slain allosaurus behind, the aviator limped onwards, doggedly following a trail which wound down, ever onwards, into the depths of the earth. Gradually the air became so filled with steam that he stripped off his fur jumper and trousers. Clad in a khaki flannel shirt, serge trousers and shoepacks, he paused long enough to count his cartridges, and found there were just fourteen. Hell! Not very many with which to venture into an unknown abyss. He distributed them in his pockets, and, somewhat relieved of the weight of the fur suit, took up his advance, playing the flashlight ahead of him as he went.

"Poor Alden," he thought. "I wonder if he's still alive?"

Every moment expecting to stumble over the mangled corpse of his friend he hurried on, making better time over the cavern floor, but soon even the lighter clothing commenced to feel oppressive.

"Must be the earth's heat," he muttered, while the steam clouds rolled by him like ghostly serpents. "Guess the crust is very thin here—something like Yellowstone. Probably I'll find some thermal springs ahead."

Just as he spoke the tunnel took a sharp turn to the right. He scrambled around the bend to stand petrified, for with the suddenness of lightning a flood of dazzling orange-red light sprang into being. Momentarily it blinded him, then revealed strange, incomprehensible scenes. It appeared that two short shafts of incandescent flame roared through transparent columns of glass on either side of the passage some fifty yards distant. Subconsciously Nelson realized that these columns began and ended in stonework that was smooth and well joined.

As his eyes became accustomed to the glare he distinguished beside each light pillar two bronze doors, some eight feet high and semicircular in shape. These had been evidently pulled back to expose the lights. Then his breath stopped in his throat, for there, standing beside them, was a gleaming group of six or eight of the strangest creatures Nelson could ever have imagined. They were men—there was no mistaking that—men of normal size, but they were so helmeted and incased in a curious type of armor that for a moment he believed them gargoyles.

Quite motionless he stood, clutching the cold barrel of the Winchester in a spasmodic grip and staring up at those two watch-towers, built like gigantic swallows' nests into sheer rock wall. He could see the warriors stationed there, peering curiously down at him from the depths of heavy, bronze helmets—helmets which in shape much resembled those of an ancient Grecian hoplite, for the nose guards and cheek pieces descended so low as to completely mask the features of those strange guards. For crests these helmets bore exquisitely wrought bronze dolphins, with brilliant blue eyes of sapphire. But what fascinated Nelson most was the curious armor they wore. Beneath breast plates of polished bronze, these strange warriors wore what seemed to be a kind of chain mail—yet it was not that, for the texture had more the appearance of some heavy but pliant leather, finished with a metallic surfacing.

Suddenly the spell of mutual amazement was broken, for a tall warrior in a breast plate that glittered with diamonds and seemed altogether more ornate than the rest, clapped a short brass horn to his lips and blew a single piercing note. At once there appeared on the tunnel's floor, not a hundred yards from the startled aviator, a rank of perhaps twenty soldiers, accoutred exactly like those he beheld by the light boxes. They came scrambling over the boulders, their shadows grotesquely preceding them. In their hands were long shafted spears, and on their left arms rectangular shields, charged with a lively dolphin in the act of swimming. Some of them, however, held short hoses in their hands, hoses that sprouted from tight brass coils strapped to their broad shoulders.

Again the commanding figure aloft raised the horn. From the tail of his eye Nelson caught the gleam of metal in the orange glare. While a blast, harsh as the scream of a fire siren, echoed and re-echoed eerily through the passage, there appeared a fresh detachment. Nelson shrank back in horror, for these bronze-armored warriors led, at the end of a powerful chain, two more of those huge, ferocious allosaurs, exactly like the one he had slain but a short while back.

Like well regulated automatons the hoplite rank opened to permit the passage of those repulsive, eager monsters, then closed up again and halted, spears levelled before them in the precise manner of an ancient Grecian phalanx, while the men with those curious hose-like contrivances ran out to guard the flanks.

"I'm done for now," thought Nelson as he threw off the Winchester's safety catch. "I suppose they'll turn those nightmares loose on me."

He was right. For all the world as though they led war dogs, the keepers in brazen armor advanced, the dull metallic clank of their accoutrement clearly discernible above the sibilant hiss of their hideous charges, which hopped along grotesquely like kangaroos, using their long and powerful tails as a counterpoise.

Then the officer watching from the left hand swallow's nest shouted a hoarse, unintelligible command, whereupon one of the keepers raised his right hand in a sharp gesture that instantly flattened the incredible monster to earth, exactly like an obedient bird dog.

As in a fantastic dream Nelson watched one of the armored guardians unsnap the hook of the powerful chain by which his allosaurus was secured. Then, whistling sharply, he clapped his hands and pointed straight at the motionless aviator. The creature's green white eyes flickered back and forth, and a chill, colder than the outer Arctic, invaded Nelson's breast as those unearthly eyes came to rest upon him.

Meanwhile the other allosaurus remained crouched, whining impatiently for its keepers to cast it loose.

Fixing burning eyes upon the American, the foremost keeper threw back his head. "Ahre-e-e!" he shouted. Instantly the freed allosaurus arose, balanced its enormous bulk, then commenced to leap forward at tremendous speed, clearing fifteen or twenty feet with each jump and uttering a curious, whistling scream as it bore down, a terrifying vision of gleaming teeth and talons.

Shaking off the paralysis of despair, Nelson whipped up the Winchester and, as before, sighted squarely between those blazing, gemlike eyes. When the huge monster was but twenty feet away he fired, and the report thundered and banged in the cavern like the crash of a summer storm. In mid-air the ghastly carnivore teemed to stagger. Its tail twitched sharply as in an effort to recover its balance. Then, quite like any normal creature that is shot through the head, it lost all sense of direction and made great convulsive leaps, around and around, clawing madly at the air, bumping into the rock walls and uttering soul-shaking shrieks of agony. Like a gargoyle gone mad it reeled back towards the startled rank of spearmen. As it came, Nelson saw the second allosaurus rear itself backwards and, balanced on its tail, strike out with powerful hind legs as its maddened fellow drew near.

Like razors the great talons ripped through the dying allosaurus' belly, exposing the gray-red intestines as the stricken creature raced by, snapping crazily at the empty air.

A single mighty sweep of the monster's tail crushed five or six of the panic-stricken keepers and guards, strewing them like broken and abandoned marionettes among the stones. Hissing and obviously terrified, the second dinosaur watched the dying struggles of its mate; then, obedient to a terrified shout from its keepers, wheeled about to join in a frantic rout of the spearmen, who, casting aside shield, spear and brass coil, fled for dear life in the direction of those invisible passages through which they had appeared.

CHAPTER II

No less amazed and alarmed than those vanished soldiers, Nelson remained rooted to the ground, conscious that in the swallow's nest overhead there remained only the officer—a tall, broad shouldered man with golden beard showing from under the cheek pieces of his helmet. Across the body of the still writhing monster their glances met. Nelson could see by the light of those strange pillars of fire that the other's eyes were blue as any Norseman's. Leaning far out over the stone parapet the other stared down upon the aviator from the depths of his jewelled helmet in a strange mixture of curiosity and awe.

Suddenly Nelson's nerves snapped and he shook a trembling fist at the martial figure above.

"Go away!" he shrieked, and reeled back on the edge of collapse. "Go away, you damn phantom! You're driving me crazy—crazy, I tell you!"

The other stiffened, then turned and, uttering a hoarse shout, vanished, leaving the noiseless and apparently heatless pillar of fire flaring steadily.

Recovering somewhat, Nelson set his teeth, advanced to the nearest corpse, stooped and regarded him who lay there, with bronze helmet fallen off.

"It's a man and not a ghost," he murmured as his finger encountered flesh that was still warm. "Red headed too, or I'm a liar. Now what in hell is all this?"

For all his bewilderment he began to feel better and his swaying reason became steadier. "Bronze, bronze—nothing but bronze," the aviator told himself as he further examined the scattered equipment. "Evidently these fellows don't know the use of iron or steel."

With increased curiosity he bent over another splendidly built dead man who lay with back broken and sightless eyes staring fixedly onto the steam current meandering silently along the cavern's roof. From the fallen man's belt were slung half a dozen curious weapons that looked not unlike potato mashers, except that they were bronze headed and had wooden handles.

"Hum," he commented, "kind of like the grenades the Boche used in the late lamented. Wonder what the devil these are?"

Suddenly his ear detected the sound of a footstep and, on looking swiftly up, he beheld that same yellow bearded officer who had directed the attack. This strange being had taken off his ponderous helmet to carry it in his left hand, while his right was held vertically in the immemorial sign of peace. On he came with powerful martial strides, a brilliant green cloak flapping gently behind him and the jewels in his brazen armor glinting like so many tiny colored eyes. The stranger was indeed handsome, Nelson noticed—and then he received perhaps the greatest shock of the whole chimerical adventure. The gold bearded man halted some twenty feet away, smiled and spoke in a curiously inflected but perfectly recognizable voice.

"Welcome to the Empire of the Atlans. Prithee, Wanderer, what be thy name?"

For a long moment Nelson was entirely too taken back to make a reply. Desperately his already perplexed brain tried to comprehend. Here was a handsome six-footer, dressed in the arms of an ancient race, speaking English of the seventeenth century!

As at a phantom, he regarded the stalwart, faintly ominous figure, from heavy leather sandals to bronze greaves, thence to wide belt from which dangled more of those curious grenadelike objects. His glance paused on the officer's beautifully wrought bronze cuirasse or breast plate which showed in relief an emerald scaled dolphin and trident. These, Nelson decided, must be the national emblems of this incomprehensible nation.

Then their eyes met, held each other a long moment until the tall officer's features, disfigured by a long red scar across the jaw, broke into a hard smile.

"Hero Giles Hudson begs thy pardon," he said, "but methought thou spoke in the language of Sir Henry Hudson, my ancestor?"

"Sir Henry Hudson!" stammered Nelson incredulously. "The old explorer whose men turned him adrift? So that's why you're talking embalmed English!" In desperation his weary brain strove to understand.

"I know naught," replied the other with a grave smile, "save that the founder of our royal line spoke what he called English. He came from the Ice World to rule wisely over Atlans. He was the greatest Atlantean of history."

"Atlantean?" echoed Nelson, while his mind groped frantically in the recess of his memory. "Atlans, Atlantis!" A great light broke upon him. "The lost Atlantis! Great God!" Had he stumbled upon a remnant of that powerful people whose fabled empire had been drowned ten centuries ago in the cold waves of the Atlantic?

"Aye," the yellow haired warrior continued as though reading his thoughts, "long centuries ago this valley was peopled by those who escaped the great cataclysm which ended the mother country. Later came another race, barbarian wanderers like thyself." He bowed for all the world like a courtly English gentleman. "But methinks thou art in need of food and sustenance?"

"You bet I'm hungry," was Nelson's emphatic reply. "I'm

one short jump of starvation and the D. T.'s. But hold on a minute," he cried. "I'm looking for a friend of mine. He went by here, didn't he?"

"Aye." A crafty expression Nelson did not like crept into Hero Giles Hudson's face as he solemnly inclined his head.

"For the nonce, fair sir, thy companion is hale and sound. I beg your patience."

With a quick gesture the Atlantean raised his dolphin-shaped horn and blew three short blasts while Nelson, in sudden alarm, cocked his rifle and brought it in line with the other's chest. The glittering officer saw the motion, but made no effort to move from the line of sights.

"Thy gesture avails naught," said he with stiff courtesy. "When Hero Giles gives his word, it stands good though Heliopolis and the Empire of the Atlans fall."

One by one half a dozen spearmen appeared, all obviously very frightened and only moved by an apparently Spartan discipline. Promptly they saluted, whereupon the Hero—as his title appeared to be—uttered a number of brief commands in some guttural language entirely unintelligible to the dazed aviator.

Presently a strange column appeared, composed of some fifteen or twenty disarmed men marching between a double rank of heavily equipped hoplites. As they drew near, they clasped imploring hands and evidently begged for mercy from the stern, tight jawed figure at Nelson's side. Contemptuous and unhearing the prisoners' piteous pleadings and lamentations, Hero Giles scowled upon them and deliberately turned his back.

"What are they?" inquired Nelson, vaguely alarmed. "Enemies?"

"Yes." There was a certain bitter savagery in the speaker's voice. "These are the dauntless defenders of Atlans who ran at the report of thy weapon. Presently they die."

It was useless to interfere. The horrified aviator knew it and watched with compassionate eyes while the condemned soldiers were ranged in a single, white faced line. They remained silent now, seeming to have found courage now that hope was dead.

Upon brief command from a subaltern, the guards wheeled about and retreated perhaps twenty yards down the passage. There they halted, glittering eyes peering through the slots in their helmets to fix themselves upon the rigid prisoners who stood numbly resigned to death.

With surprising speed each member of that weird firing squad detached a brazen grenade from his belt, then threw back his arm in exactly the same attitude as a bomb-throwing doughboy. Then there came a short, sharp command and some fifteen or twenty grenades bobbed through the air to crash on the stones at the feet of the victims.

His head swimming with repulsion at the slaughter, Nelson beheld a curious sight. It seemed that from the broken grenades appeared a yellowish green vapor which sprung *of its own accord* upon the silent upright rank! In an instant it settled like falling snow upon the doomed soldiers. For a breathless fraction of a second they stood, eyes wide with horror, then collapsed, kicking and struggling as men do under the influence of gas.

"Horrible!" gasped Nelson. "What was in the bombs?"

"A vapor," explained Hero Giles shortly. "A fungus vapor which, falling upon exposed flesh, instantly invades the blood and multiplies by millions. See—" He pointed to the nearest dead man and Nelson, with starting eyes, watched a yellowish growth commencing to sprout from the dead man's nostrils. Swiftly the poisonous mould threw out tiny branches, spreading with astounding rapidity over the skin until, in less than a minute after the grenades had exploded, the whole tumbled heap of dead were covered with a horrible yellow green fungus growth.

"Thou seest?" Hero Giles demanded. "Powerful, is it not? It is against the fungus vapor we wear this body armor made from the skin of a small lizard which inhabits our mountains."

Shocked and appalled, Nelson watched the retreat of the solemn, silent execution party.

Other soldiers fell to unconcernedly stripping their fallen comrades of equipment; then, to Nelson's horrified surprise, two hideous allosauri reappeared, shepherded by some six or eight keepers. Once the horrible creatures were released, they pounced upon the dead and, snarling horribly, commenced to rend and devour the corpses.

Too shaken to comment or to make the protest he knew to be futile, Nelson followed the stalwart English-speaking officer into a bronze door set in the cavern wall and up a short flight of stairs into what appeared to be a guard room, where food and wine were immediately set before the famished aviator.

"Yea," Hero Giles was saying as he set down a beautiful goblet and wiped the last traces of wine from his beard, "we will soon o'ertake thy friend. He was but little hurt, and thou wilt assuredly join him in judgment before our great Emperor, Altorius XXII, at Heliopolis, our capital."

"Heliopolis?" mumbled Nelson, his mouth full of delicious stew that seemed to be made of veal. "Heliopolis? How far away is it?"

"A hundred leagues more or less," the other smiled. "Almost a third of the distance up this great valley."

"One hundred leagues! Three hundred miles! Then we won't be there for several days."

The Hero's deep, rather ominous laughter rang out in the little rock hewn chamber. "Days?" he jeered. "Days? Art thou mad? In two hours from the time we board the tube-road thou shalt learn thy fate from his Serene Highness."

"What!" Nelson's sunken and blood-shot gray eyes widened, while his jaw dropped incredulously. "One hundred leagues in two hours? As I remember there are about three miles to a league, so a hundred leagues in two hours means one hundred and fifty miles an hour! Why, that's utterly impossible! The Twentieth Century Limited doesn't go half so fast."

Several enormous emeralds set into the other's bronze cuirasse glittered softly and the Hero's cold blue eyes hardened as his hand sought the grenade belt.

"Impossible? Dost doubt my words, sirrah?" With an effort he controlled himself. "Nay, thou shalt see for thyself ere long. The tube-road runs from Heracles to Heliopolis. Thou canst trace its course on this map here on the wall."

"The dog-born devils of Jarmuth have no such means of travel," continued the Atlantean, with a touch of smug pride that reminded Nelson of a small town Middle Westerner speaking of the "rightest, tightest little town west of the Mississippi."

Nelson found it extremely weird to be sitting there in a heavy arm chair, drinking good red wine with a fierce armor-clad warrior who wore sandals, sword and a war cloak such as might have graced the limbs of Alexander of Macedon. But with the food and rich warm wine, he felt blood, strength and self-confidence pouring back into his weary body. "Jarmuth?" he inquired. "What is Jarmuth?"

At his question the domineering, predatory face across the table darkened and the scar on his cheek flamed red as a scowl of hatred gripped Hero Giles' visage.

"Jarmuth!" snarled the Hero, and his great hand closed like a vise. "Jarmuth! A nation of treacherous, gold-adoring cannibals, whose countless hordes, spawned in the hot lowlands, ever threaten our frontiers. I tell thee, Friend Nelson, the dog-sired Jereboam will not rest until mighty Heliopolis lies in a heap of smoking ashes."

"Evidently," thought Nelson, taken aback at the other's vehemence, "this lad's English only in speech. I guess he's all Atlantean outside of that."

Warming to a fiercer pitch, the other fixed his guest with a smoldering gaze. "Jarmuth lies beyond Apidanus, the boiling river, and is the home of a savage horde whose horrid rites in Jezreel, the capital, stink as an offense to Saturn and the High Gods! Why, mark you," the warrior prince continued, interrupting his tirade to gulp a goblet of wine, "five years ago, by treachery, they seized the beauteous Altara, sister of our gracious Emperor, and upon the annual feast of Beelzebub, that vile demon they worship, the dark dogs would have sacrificed and devoured her, according to their rites, had not our Emperor dispatched a ransom of six fair maidens to take her place.

"Every year since then Jereboam has exacted that same tribute. Every year their princes and priests gorge themselves on the tender white flesh of our fairest and noblest maidens. But this tribute must end! The augurs have told us so. Help will come from the Ice World." Hero Giles brought crashing down on the table a brawny fist, on whose wrist was fixed a bright, gem-studded bracelet.

Horror-stricken, Nelson nodded.

"It is for this alone," continued the Hero somberly, "that thy life and that of thy friend have been spared."

"So? I didn't notice," broke in Nelson, "that you particularly went out of your way to preserve my health a while back."

The heavy golden head shook slowly and a grim smile played about those thin cruel lips. "Nay, but I could have had thee slain. Come, as we go to the tube-road I'll show thee how much thou liest in the hollow of this, my hand." He thrust out a broad, powerful palm. "Forget not, fair sir. At any moment I or my Imperial Master may choose to close that hand."

"Perhaps!" stated Nelson, feeling it imperative to keep up his pose of independence. "But it might just happen that your hand would close on a porcupine, and so far from hurting the porcupine it would be your hand that would be hurt."

"Sirrah!" The Atlantean sprang to his feet and one hand shot to the grip of his ponderous, bronze sword; but even more quickly Nelson snatched up his rifle, a thin smile playing on his lips.

"Drop it," he snapped. "Control yourself, or I'll plug you like that allosaur. Be reasonable, can't you? We both want something, and perhaps can help each other gain it."

The taut, menacing figure in armor relaxed and, with a gentle clank of accoutrement, Hero Giles resumed his seat.

"Prithee pardon me," he apologized ungraciously. "I was ever a hot-head and there is much in what thou sayest. We wish to force an end to this annual tribute—if not to regain our beloved Altara. And thou"—his heavy, golden eyebrows shot up—"and thou, what dost thou wish?"

Nelson lowered the menacing barrel. "I want the return of Richard Alden, free passage back to that spot where he was captured and plenty of food and help should we need it. If I aid you in one, you must promise me in the other."

"Aye," returned the other doubtfully. "But I myself can pledge naught save thy immediate safety. 'Tis for our Imperial Majesty to say whether both thou and thy friend shall live, or whether ye shall feed our war dogs. Come now, we must go to Heliopolis."

Map of Jarmuth and Atlans

Picking up his heavy, bronze helmet the Atlantean prince set it on his yellow head and waited impatiently for Nelson to drain the last of his wine. Then, with a swirl of his green cloak, he vanished through the rock wall, closely followed by a singularly distracted and alarmed aviator.

CHAPTER III

A bright yellow glare steadily increased to mark the end of the tunnel down which the two had progressed; then, with the sharp abruptness of a hand-clap, there resounded a loud challenge in that unintelligible Atlantean language, above which the hiss of steam could be loudly heard.

Instantly the Atlantean prince strode forward, a commanding figure. Momentarily his helmet and the dangling grenadelike bombs were sharply outlined against that unearthly yellow light. He raised his hand and dropped it, palm outward, to his chin in what must have been a salute. The hissing sound of steam then faded into silence.

Followed at a respectful distance by a pair of silent, bronze-helmeted hoplites, Nelson and his guide descended a narrow stair, which broadened at the base. It was a very long staircase composed of perhaps two or three hundred steps which were occasionally interrupted by wide stone terraces. On these level spaces were fixed what appeared to be enormous field guns of glittering brass. They were similar, yet somehow oddly dissimilar, to the great guns Nelson had seen in France.

"Behold, oh Wanderer," Hero Giles declaimed impressively, "the lands of Atlans and Jarmuth!"

It was a weird landscape that met Nelson's half unbelieving gaze, a landscape green with that brilliance peculiar to spring meadows, lying beneath the same deep blue sky that overarched the surrounding barren ice fields which hemmed in this astounding valley.

A slight smile played over Hero Giles' thin lips as he watched the amazed aviator.

"The splendor of our country must indeed astound thee,"

he observed, "having come from the dreary fastness of the outer Ice World. But come; we are now to pass the great retortii guarding the entrance into the valley."

Nelson's eyes turned again to the weapons that so oddly resembled field guns. He examined them closely, inspecting them narrowly for the differences he knew must exist between them and the artillery that had thundered during the War of the Nations.

The chief difference lay in the mounting of these starkly beautiful weapons. They seemed to be fixed on a movable pivot set into the coal black rock itself. Like modern artillery, these curious pieces of ordnance bore a bronze shield to protect their crews, through which projected the long and very narrow barrels of the guns. Grouped like cannoneers about their piece stood various red-crested Atlantean artillerymen. At a glance Nelson recognized the difference in their equipment from that of the spearmen behind them. These former bore no shields, no swords or bombs, but wore that same kind of leather body-armor which graced the powerful limbs of Hero Giles. Their helmets, too, were different: only the dolphin crest with a tuft of red feathers spouting from it bore any resemblance to those of the infantry, and, moreover, the artillerymen's eyes were shielded by goggles with thick blue lenses.

As the Hero approached, officers among them saluted, then sank on one knee with head humbly bent.

"Rather odd looking guns," commented Nelson. "I'm not much of an artilleryman, but I'm wondering how you take up the recoil?"

The Atlantean's laugh, which always reminded his guest of the purr of a tiger, rang out. "Why, marry, good sir, there is no recoil! These guns do not use that powder which Sir

Henry, founder of our line, did speak of. Thou wouldst see one fired?"

His curiosity immeasurably piqued, Nelson nodded, whereupon the Atlantean wheeled about and barked a brief command. With truly Prussian precision, the artillerymen sprang to their posts, some to a series of levers which sprouted from the rock platform without any apparent connection, and some to wheels and gauges of varying size that clustered in bewildering intricacy about the breech of the great brass gun.

"Markest thou that tree yonder, on the ledge of the valley?" The Atlantean's blunt outstretched finger indicated a towering pine sprouting from among a mass of reddish volcanic rock at the rim of that new world.

"Yes, I see it, but—" Nelson was astounded. A pine tree in the upper Arctic! That alone was sufficient cause for amazement. From a stiff red-plumed gun captain issued a brief series of commands which set the wonderfully drilled crew to silently adjusting their training and elevating mechanism. Click! Clack! Sis-s-s-s!

All up and down the vast staircase other gun crews stood watching. Nelson saw their weird, bluish goggles raised to that platform where, for all the world like a coast defense howitzer, the great cannon swung majestically about on the ponderous, brazen column which seemed to support it. Gradually the muzzle was elevated, then traversed a few feet, to finally come to a halt.

"Jakul, a Hero!" shouted the gun captain, his hand raised to Hero Giles.

"Thou art ready, Friend Nelson?" he inquired in tolerant amusement. "Mark well yon pine tree!

"Storr!"

Nelson saw one of the armored cannoneers bend

forward, firmly grasp a short lever with both hands. In anticipation of a terrific report, the aviator pressed finger tips to his ears. There followed not a thundering crash, but a curious, eery, high-pitched scream, rather like that of a fire siren. There was no smoke! Nelson's incredulous eyes sought the muzzle of the gun and detected issuing from it what appeared to be a thin, white rod. This shimmering stream of silver shot straight towards the pine tree, gradually widening and giving off feathery billows of steam. In a fraction of a moment the target was completely veiled from sight in a furious pall of clouds which, to Nelson's great astonishment, did not dissipate nor condense with the speed of ordinary steam.

"Nava!"

With impressive suddenness the screaming sound faded, leaving a sort of stunned silence on the gun platform. The gunners stalked back to their original stations.

Slowly, reluctantly, the mist enveloping the pine tree cleared away and Nelson felt a chill creeping up his spine. The pine was a good three hundred yards away, yet now it sagged limp to earth, stripped of bark, twigs and needles, only the bright yellow trunk and major branches remaining.

"That tree was a good two feet thick," mused the astounded aviator, "yet the steam gun bent it like a sapling. My God! What would it do to a man?"

"What thinkest thou of our retortii?" The Atlantean's beard glinted like metal as he shook with a grim, silent laughter. "These great retortii can shoot half a league and will blast any living thing in their path. I tell thee, friend Nelson, the discharge of even a small retortii will strip the flesh from a man's bones as a peasant strips the husk from an ear of corn!"

"Fearful, terrible!" was Nelson's awed comment. "Is there no defence against them?"

"Of course." The Hero's green feather-crested helmet gleamed with a nod. "Was there ever an instrument of war that had not its defence? Yea, we have the blue vapor to shatter steam particles—it is called the blue maxima. Thou wilt presently see some of our troops armed with it."

"But where does this steam come from? How is it generated?" These two were the first of a host of questions which trembled on Nelson's lips.

"The steam," replied the Atlantean, "comes from the earth. We compress it many times, then feed it into our retortii. Without the heat of Mother Earth and our flame suns we would all perish. Steam is our motive power, our defence and our enemy!"

He flung his hand towards the vast valley stretched before them. It was hemmed in on either side by colossal breath-taking mountain ranges, whose caps shone and glittered with an eternal snow.

"Some foothills! They must rise all of 25,000 feet from the valley floor," decided the aviator, "and I should imagine this valley is a good mile below sea level. Yes! That must be it: this nightmare country lies in a huge geographical fault—something like the Dead Sea."

Mile after mile he could see fertile green land stretching away toward some low undulating hills on the horizon. Atlans was very thickly settled—that he recognized at once—for the terrain was divided and sub-divided into a vast checker-board, such as he had seen in France and

Germany, while terraces, green with produce, had been laboriously gouged out of the frowning mountain sides.

Then his eye encountered the source of that curious amber light which pervaded the whole valley. A titanic flaming gas vent spouted like a cyclopean torch from the peak of a nearby mountain. Its steady, subdued roar struck Nelson's ear as he turned away his eyes, for the glare was too intense to be long endured. Further down the valley were two more such incandescent vents, shooting their flaming tongues boldly into the sky, warming the air and casting that rich, amber radiance over all.

"That is Mount Ossa nearest us," the Atlantean's voice came as though from a long distance. Victor Nelson was too staggered, too unspeakably amazed to register the fact of the Hero's proximity. "Below are Pelion and Jilboa, which, with Jabor, the greatest of all the flames, illuminate and warm the valley."

Nelson's eye, trained to be all observant, ranged far and wide, noting the presence of many lacy, frothing geysers which spouted at varying intervals. There were, also, many steaming ponds and waterfalls which sprang in smoky confusion from the rock palisades to either side.

Nearer at hand he could distinguish a number of huge stone structures, evidently forts and public buildings. Strategically placed all about were more of those terrible brass retortii, gleaming dully under the incandescent glare of the flame sun.

"Come," cried Hero Giles with an impatient gesture of his hand, "we must e'en hasten to the tube-road terminal. Word has long since been sent to Heliopolis of thy arrival."

Downwards into the valley, which grew ever warmer and more fertile, the Atlantean led on, explaining a thousand and one details to the astounded aviator. Presently they approached the nearest of the great stone structures and Nelson received yet another shock. In a courtyard was drilling what would correspond to a troop of cavalry in the outer world. In orderly ranks the troopers wheeled, marched and counter-marched, their brazen armor twinkling and clashing softly as they carried out their evolutions with an amazing precision. But what astonished Nelson was the fact that each of these strange troopers bestrode a lithe, long-limbed variety of dinosaur, a good half smaller than the allosauri he had encountered in the tunnel. These agile creatures ran about on their hind legs with astonishing speed, using a long reptilian tail as a balance.

On the back of each trooper was fastened a compact circular copper tank, from which sprouted a flexible metal hose that ended in what looked like a ponderous type of pistol.

In distinction to the red of the artillerymen and the blue of the Hoplites, these curious cavalrymen wore brilliant crests of yellow feathers, and from their lance tips fluttered tiny pennons of that same color.

"They must travel at least as fast as a race horse," decided the aviator after studying the swift evolutions of the scaly chargers. To his ears came the curious dry scrape and rattle of their horny claws on the stone pavement of the drill yard.

He would have lingered to see more, for those grotesque, lizard-like chargers interested him immensely, but Hero Giles beckoned imperiously. So, dropping the Winchester to the hollow of his arm, Nelson followed him into the brilliantly gas-lit depths of the great structure.

Everywhere were red bearded, white skinned soldiers, staring at him with the frank curiosity of children. Powerful, magnificently built fellows they were, all in uniforms of different designs.

The walls about him, Nelson noticed, were covered with really beautiful friezes depicting various warlike scenes in that pure beauty of proportion found only in ancient Grecian temples.

On and on through resounding tunnels, past busy markets and barracks, hurried the two travelers. Then the Atlantean halted before a gracefully arched doorway where stood two hoplites, who immediately lowered spears to bar the passage. At a word from Hero Giles, however, they saluted and fell back in position—immovable, grim guardians.

Inside was a short staircase, beautifully wrought of bronze. Up this flashed the Atlantean's mail-clad body; then he came to a halt under the direct rays of a blinding light.

Nelson, on arriving above, discovered that the chamber was lined with jointless brass about ten feet high and circular in shape. "What's this?" he demanded curiously.

"The terminal of the tube-road. In a moment thou shalt see the great cylinder arrive."

The words were hardly by the Hero's lips when there appeared, noiselessly and amid a great rush of air, a huge metal cylinder that ran upon a sort of truck. It rumbled up to the edge of the platform and from its end a small door was opened.

Hero Giles exchanged a few sentences with an elderly man who appeared to act as control master, then he indicated the glowing doorway of the cylinder.

Firmly clutching his Winchester, Nelson bowed his head and stepped inside, there to discover a luxury he had never anticipated. The interior of the cylinder was brilliantly lit and on both sides were ranged wide divans, strewn with many silken cushions. In a rack nearby were several graceful glass amphora, filled with red and tawny wine.

"The cylinder must be about thirty feet long," the marvelling American told himself, "and about ten feet in diameter. Guess it works on the same principle as the compressed air tubes the department stores use to send change with."

Gingerly he tested the nearest divan and marvelled at the curious softness of what appeared to be a gigantic tiger skin. Meanwhile Hero Giles entered, his stern features even more serious, but with him was a younger man who resembled him not a little.

"Fair brother," said the Atlantean to his companion, "this is he of whom I spoke. Friend Nelson, this is Hero John, my next youngest brother—he, too, speaks the language of the great Sir Henry Hudson."

The metallic clang of the door being shut brought a sharp qualm to Nelson's heart. "What are they doing?" he demanded quickly.

"The menials bolt the door beyond," explained Hero Giles with amused gravity. "In a moment our cylinder will be placed in the dispatching chamber, where steam pressure will be exerted. We shall then be hurled through this vacuum tube-road to Heliopolis, greatest city of Atlans. In an hour we will be there."

Outside sounded the sudden insistent clangor of a gong, and immediately the hiss of steam grew louder. The car shuddered as the hissing rose to an eery scream, then all at once the cylinder leaped forward, nearly hurling Nelson from his seat. He struggled as best he might to gain his equilibrium, for the eyes of the others were on him.

Then, more smoothly, the great cylinder gathered speed and hurtled on through the darkness of the tube-road towards Heliopolis, where Victor Nelson would read the book of Fate.

CHAPTER IV

On the arrival platform at Heliopolis reigned a fierce excitement. Nelson noted countless armed and unarmed warriors hurrying to and fro, desperately intent on reaching their various posts, and snarling ill-temperedly as they elbowed their fellows aside. As soon as they appeared, Hero Giles and his brother became the center of an excited press of gorgeously armored officers.

"Hum!" murmured the aviator under his breath. "Something's happened. Must be a revolution, an earthquake or a Democratic convention in town; these boys seem all steamed up."

Intently he studied the ring of fierce, red bearded faces surrounding his late hosts and gathered that indeed some event of overwhelming importance had taken place. Presently a splendid falcon-eyed old man in a yellow cloak strode up, struggling to control himself. His resemblance to the two Heroes struck Nelson immediately.

"Harken ye," he cried, in that Elizabethan English which appeared to be the hieratic language of the New Atlantis' rulers. "Have ye heard? The dog-conceived sons of Semites have broken the truce! But three measures gone by, a brigade of their mounted podokesons swooped down on this very suburb of Tricca, yea, to the very gates of Heliopolis! The foul man-eating dogs slaughtered royal serfs and burnt two quarters of the suburb to the ground! Moreover, they seized that prisoner"—Nelson's heart gave a great leap at the word—"whom thou sentest from the mountain passes."

"What!" In two swift strides Nelson was before the gray beard, his blood-shot eyes blazing with a strange light.

"What did you say about that prisoner?"

Yhe old man, who had obviously not noticed Nelson's presence, was thunderstruck to hear him speak in English until Hero Giles briefly explained his presence.

"Yea!" continued the elder, flinging lamentations furiously over his shoulder, "these swine of the Lost Tribes captured him and slew his escort. They have retreated towards the Apidanus, slaying, burning and pillaging as they go."

A sickening, deadly fear gripped the weary aviator. This was too much! Bad as it was to have Richard Alden captured by these weird descendants of a long vanished race, it was far worse to have him fall into the hands of their deadly enemies, the Jarmuthians, decadent survivors of Israel's Five Lost Tribes. The possibility of a rescue now seemed hopelessly and crushingly vague and distant. What could he do now?

In dread despair he glanced about, amazed at the prodigious numbers of scowling men who hurried by, obviously intent upon the commencement of a campaign for revenge.

Then Hero Giles turned his scarred, warlike face, now set in granite lines. "Come, Friend Nelson, my uncle Anthony bids me take thee direct to the presence of His Serene Splendor, where he lies encamped at Cierum, by the shores of Lake Copias. There he marshals the army of Atlans for a march through the hot country on Jezreel. I tell thee, thou hast come in stirring times. From Heraclea, Thebes, Ys and Mayda will come the Phalanxes. Once and forever we will deal the dogs of Jarmuth a final blow."

Victor Nelson never forgot the hours that followed. Issuing at a fast trot from the tube-road terminal, the two Heroes led the way to a vast structure, in which were stabled both the terrific allosauri and the podokesauri, those swift dinosaurs which seemed to serve the Atlanteans as horses. The dreadful hiss and snarl of these monsters resounded in his ears long before the stables came in sight, and that curious musky odor he had noted in the tunnel was sickeningly strong.

Everywhere he read signs of hurried preparations for war. Savage, surly allosauri were led from their stables, one by one, long necks writhing snakelike backwards and forwards. Then their keepers would, after a moment's tussle, secure huge leather muzzles over their gaping jaws, and the huge reptiles would be led waddling along on their hind legs out into a vast courtyard, there to hiss and strike at their nearest fellows.

"Thinkest thou couldst ride a podoko?" inquired Hero John, an anxious look on his handsome, friendly features. "They are difficult to manage—but swift in flight as the birds themselves!"

"I don't know," replied the aviator, "but I'm damn well going to try. If your Emperor can help me rescue Alden, the sooner we get started, the better."

For all his brave resolutions, his heart sank, as the green kilted keeper led forth three podokesauri. Nelson stared curiously at them as, hopping along, they drew near, to bare needle-sharp teeth at him while, brazen stirrups on either side jangled softly against their rough, scaly hides.

In evident high spirits the beasts snuffed the air and pawed with their tiny front legs excitedly, making their sharp talons glisten like polished steel. A bridle dangled from the mouth of each and a ring set in the thick upper lip served as a further means of control.

At a sharp "*Oya!*" from an old and toothless keeper,

the first podoko sank flat to the stone floor like a kneeling camel.

"A sturdy beast," commented Hero Giles, tightening his belt and securing the clasps to the emerald-green war cloak. "Here, Friend Nelson, thou hadst best don a helmet; the podokos on occasion throw back their heads and so might wound thee." So saying, he set foot in stirrup and swung up into a saddle which was built up high in the cantle to correct the sharp downward slope of the reptile's muscular back.

At a signal, Hero Giles' ugly mount rose to its height and shuffled awkwardly sidewise, as the old keeper, his eyes very wide and curious, led forward Nelson's charger.

"Look," said Hero John with a reassuring smile. "The chin strap buckles so—be sure it fits snug, else it will pound on thy head to the podoko's stride. If thou wouldst turn to the left, pull the rein so, to the right so, and if thou wouldst stop, pull strongly on the nose ring; 'tis not so difficult." He laid a friendly hand on Nelson's flannel clad shoulder. "How wilt thou manage thy curious weapon?" he inquired doubtfully. "Perhaps thou hadst best leave it behind."

There was a grim smile on Nelson's weary and wind burned features. "Not on your life, old son! This Winchester and I stick closer together than the Siamese twins."

Nelson thrust his foot into a heavy stirrup, eased his weight into the high peaked saddle and gripped the pommel, for though an excellent horseman, he had no clue as to what motion would ensue. It was wise he did so, for the podoko reared suddenly, almost flinging his rider from the saddle.

Immediately Hero John mounted, raised his right hand and dealt his podoko a stinging slap on the fore-shoulder.

The great reptile hissed in protest, but commenced to walk off with an awkward, hopping step. Nelson's mount followed suit.

Faster and faster ran the podokos, their long and scale-covered necks stretched far out ahead while their tails lifted correspondingly, much like that of an airplane about to take off.

"Whew! He must be doing all of forty-five," gasped Nelson, while the wind whistled about his ears and snapped madly at the yellow crest of his brazen helmet.

The ride which ensued remained forever fixed in the aviator's memory. Like so many shots from a gun the three podokos darted off out of the stables, past a gate guarded by a battery of retortii, whose red plumed cannoneers sprang to attention as the three strangely assorted riders sped out into the amber, perpetual light of Atlans.

Nelson, on finding his balance, looked about him to receive impressions of immensely tall structures, of pyramids which, like the ziggurats of Sumaria, and Babylon, were surmounted with beautifully proportioned temples.

"Must be at least a million people in this burg of Heliopolis," thought Nelson, easing his Winchester.

Hour after hour they sped along, frequently overtaking detachments of troops. Twice they halted to change mounts, though the podokos seemed quite tireless.

At the end of five hours' furious riding, Nelson beheld a dense white cloud low on the horizon.

"What's that?" he demanded. "Fog?"

"No," Hero John informed him. "Yonder flows the Apidanus, the boiling river. Not far away to the left lies the frontier fortress of Cierum, where is encamped the Emperor, who will sit in judgment upon thee."

Nelson's heart sank. He had been so occupied with his

fears for Alden that he had not dwelt upon his own precarious position.

Scarcely half an hour elapsed, if Nelson's wrist watch were running correctly, before he reached the tremendous, swarming camp of Altorius XXII, Emperor of Atlans. Hero Giles proved to be a powerful talisman, for everywhere officers and men alike saluted respectfully and sank on one knee as he passed.

"Wait here," he snapped, as the podokos sank obediently to the dust. "Brother John, do thou guard Friend Nelson while I seek permission of His Serene Splendor to bring the Wanderer into the Presence."

Almost immediately the elder Atlantean returned, a frown on his scarred, rather brutal visage. "Come," he muttered, "but I fear for thee, Friend Nelson; His Splendor is in a savage mood—this raid hath stirred his ire beyond all bounds."

"Nothing like cheering up a patient before he goes into the operating room," thought Nelson, and quietly threw off the safety on his Winchester. "Six shots," he reflected. "Well, if I go, I reckon I'll take some damn good company along."

The aviator was led down a long passage, at every ten feet of which was posted an enormous scowling guard, whose spears, retortii and armor were painted a brilliant jade-green. Then a musical, deep-toned gong boomed twice, and Hero Giles halted before an exquisitely wrought door, which, without any apparent propulsion, silently slid back into the massive stone walls, revealing a huge, brilliantly lit circular chamber that was hung with emerald-green hangings. In the center, surrounded by a royal guard of nobles in splendidly jeweled armor, was reared a dais, upon which stood a throne that blazed with the most varied collection of diamonds that Nelson could ever have imagined.

"Down on your face," rasped Hero Giles as, in common with his brother, he knelt and then fell prostrate on the cool black marble floor.

"Damned if I will," murmured Nelson, and remained erect.

Bolt upright, he looked across the interval and found himself staring into the furious eyes of one of the handsomest men he had ever beheld. Gripping his Winchester in a kind of "port arms" position, he stood to attention— by some curious kink of the brain reverting to his military days. And so the two men, different as day and night, faced each other. Altorius XXII clad in robes of scarlet, and a glittering cuirasse that glowed like the evening sun. His yellow head was truly splendid, reminiscent of that of a young Roman Emperor. The hair, like that of the Hudsonian Heroes, was blond, curly and close cropped. Yes, thought the awed but self-contained American, there was something genuinely imperial about the Emperor's aquiline visage, for a high intelligent forehead and piercing blue eyes dominated a strong mouth, which was marred by a decidedly cruel twist at the corners. On him, also, was set the stamp of Sir Henry Hudson's dauntless race.

"Put him is a business suit and a soft gray hat," mused Nelson, "and you would find a dozen like him in any of London's best clubs."

"Down on thy face, sirrah!" Outraged, the Emperor's voice rang like the peal of a brazen trumpet through the great pillared audience chamber. The nearest guardsmen held themselves ready, hand on sword hilt.

"No." Nelson's shaggy black head went back as he found his tongue at last. "No, Your Majesty. In America we have our own way of showing respect for authority. I'm an American and, with all respect, I'll salute you as one."

So saying, his hand flicked up in a sharp military salute to the visor of that Atlantean helmet which he still wore.

"All damn foolishness," he silently told himself. "I feel like the lead in a ten, twenty, thirty melodrama. But I suppose it's got to be done."

The Emperor's teeth gleamed in a half snarl as he sprang with Jovian wrath to his feet.

"Dog! How darest thou bandy words with us?"

"Have mercy!" hoarsely pleaded Hero John as he lay on the floor. "Have mercy, oh Splendor! He is but an ignorant wanderer from the Ice World."

It appeared that the young Hero was something of a favorite, for the masterful, thunder-browed Emperor checked himself and, still glowering, settled back on the diamond throne.

"Ye have my permission to enter and approach."

Whereupon, Hero Giles arose and, with many black looks at his guest, strode forward to briefly explain his presence.

Nelson felt Altorius' blazing blue eyes search his face.

"Then he whom the dog-born Jereboam captured was thy friend?"

"Yes," replied Nelson with dignity, "my best friend. Alden and I have traveled and wandered all over the world together."

"Over the world? The Ice World?" Altorius seemed interested, for he leaned forward, muscle corded arms very brown against the frosty brilliance of the stones studding his throne. He flipped back a scarlet cloak and bent a searching look on the straight, unafraid figure below.

Impatient to reach a decision, Nelson forebore to amplify the Emperor's assumption that the outside world was all ice and snow.

"Yes," he said, "from the land of America. I've spoken with Hero Giles, Your Majesty's Captain-General."

"So, then, no doubt, he has told you of the law of our country?" Altorius' white teeth shown again in the depths of his short, curling beard.

"Perhaps." Nelson was vague, wishing no further amplification.

"The law of Atlans," pronounced the Emperor with a frown, "states that a stranger must prove his worth to the State, else he must be put to death. Thank thou thy gods that thou hast not fallen into the hands of the Lost Tribes, for assuredly thou would perish miserably, as must thy comrade."

"What is the law of Jarmuth?" inquired Nelson, his mind furiously at work.

"Their law states that the stranger within their gates must perish on the altar of Beelzebub, Jarmuth's blood-hungry demon god." A momentary expression of sadness crept into the Emperor's blue eyes and he beat a square, powerful hand on the arm of his throne. "Aye, blood-hungry! Lack-a-day! But yesterday, six of our fairest maidens crossed the boiling river, never to return."

Nelson was about to speak when from outside came the blast of a trumpet. The assembled Atlanteans started, paused, and remained silent, listening intently.

Hero Giles looked up, a light kindling in his deep-set eyes. "Yon was an Israelite trumpet."

As the words left his lips there came a hurried rapping at the portal, whereupon the guards sprang forward.

"Bid them enter." Altorius seemed strangely tense and uneasy.

Quietly the door rolled back as before, revealing an Atlantean whose eyes rolled with alarm. He hurried forward and flung himself on the floor at the Emperor's sandaled feet.

"Harken, oh Serene Splendor! Waiting without is an embassy from his Majesty of Jarmuth. They bear words for thine Imperial Highness."

"Now, by Saturn! Here's insolence—at an hour such as this!" With a furious swirl of his scarlet cloak Altorius leaped to his feet, hand on the ivory handle of his sword, which, to Nelson's amusement was not of bronze, but of good, blue-gray steel.

"I'll bet it's old Sir Henry's original pet sticker," he thought.

"Bring on these dogs of Israel," growled Altorius. "They shall die!"

"Gently, gently, oh Splendor," murmured Hero John. "Our full force is not yet camped on the Plains of Poseidon."

"Nay! Have the rogues flayed alive!" was the advice of the hot-headed elder brother. He, like the Emperor, was scowling and livid with fury.

Presently there appeared four men, stalwart warriors as totally different in aspect from the Atlanteans as humans might be. The two races were alike only in splendid physical proportions and human figures. They, the Jarmuthians, were black haired and dark skinned, whereas the Atlanteans, with the exception of Sir Henry's progeny, were red headed. Truculently the half naked ambassadors strode over the polished floor, which reflected their rude images. Their hairy chests, arms and legs afforded a sharp contrast to the neat Atlantean nobles, who drew back with expressions of disgust.

"Good God!" gasped Nelson in lively surprise. "A bunch of the boys from Seventh Avenue!"

It was true: each Jarmuthian clearly betrayed his Hebraic origin in huge, fleshy nose and pendulous lower lip, so characteristic of the Semitic race. They were fierce, shaggy fellows, naked from the waist up save for a kind of jointed body armor, reminiscent of a Roman legionnaire's. Their long abundant blue-black hair was either plaited or flowed uncut over splendidly muscled shoulders. Their beards on the other hand were short and frizzed into tight curls, in the Assyrian manner. On each man's head was set a highly polished, pointed casque of copper, surmounted in each instance by the six-pointed star of Solomon. Otherwise the brutal looking emissaries wore nothing but dirty, food-spotted kilts and rough hide sandals secured by thongs.

With all the insolence and self assurance of conquerors in the presence of slaves the four jet-eyed ambassadors swaggered up to the diamond throne. Then the foremost briefly inclined his head towards Altorius in a grudging salute and began to speak in deep, resonant tones.

From that point Nelson could understand nothing of the conversation as it was carried on in the guttural and unintelligible language of that lost realm, but, from time to time Hero John found opportunity to translate an occasional phrase.

Darker and darker grew the brows of the gorgeously attired Emperor and his eagle-visaged Captain-General as they listened to the pompous oratory of the foremost Jarmuthian, and in dark fury more than one Atlantean noble half drew his sword when the speaker fell silent at last.

"He said," the younger Atlantean whispered, "that Jereboam is no longer satisfied with six maidens. Beelzebub demands a further offering of six more damsels to be delivered before the third division of time on the morrow. By Saturn! The insolence of these besotted swine passes all tolerance!"

From the Atlantean Emperor's outraged negative gestures, Nelson surmised that Altorius was making an emphatic refusal and even adding some vicious threat. The foremost Jarmuthian slapped huge dirty hands on armored hips and fell to laughing with an insolence that would have provoked a rabbit.

Forgetting dignity and self-control, Altorius, in a single tigerish leap sprang from his throne and knocked the mocker senseless with a powerful blow to the jaw. Then, spurning the fallen Jarmuthian with a sandaled foot, the Atlantean fixed blazing eyes upon the three other ambassadors who, nothing daunted, closed up, muttering savagely in their frizzed black beards, while their hands sought the spot where swords would normally have hung.

"Nice right to the jaw," commented Nelson with a grin. "He's still English enough to use his fists." He turned to Hero John, who stood with an expression of horror on his comely features. "What caused the row?"

"Verily, our plight is grave indeed. That braggart dog threatened to march on Heliopolis in the first division of morning, and,"—Hero John's lips compressed into a hopeless, taut expression—"our reinforcing phalanxes can never arrive in time to defend Cierum at that hour. Should the defense fail, as it must—since they outnumber us three to one for the nonce—it would cost us many thousands of men to stay the blood-hungry hordes of Jereboam once freed on the great plain."

Like a star shell bursting on a cloudy night came the inception of an idea.

"Here," cried Nelson, "I've an idea! Maybe I can fix a stall until the rest of your boys do a General Phil Sheridan and get here."

Hero John's blue eyes widened uncomprehendingly. "What?" he demanded. "What dost thou propose?"

Nelson's hand crept to his head, for the unaccustomed weight and heat of the helmet made it itch. "You say these bright boys from over the border want to chow six more girls? Am I right?"

"Yea, oh Friend Nelson, they demand the victims tomorrow morn, else they advance."

"All right." Nelson was thinking fast now, a dreadful vision of Richard Alden stretched for sacrifice on the brass altar of Beelzebub ever floating before his aching eyes. "Tell those Semites that they can have those six girls *if* they can take them away from me."

A puzzled frown creased the younger Hero's brow and he tugged thoughtfully at his scant yellow beard. "Prithee pardon me, but I do not comprehend."

"All right, get this now! Tell the Jarmuthians that they can send six of their biggest and best scrappers, one for each girl. If they can take any one of those girls away from me, they take them all—taking me as well—and we'll all get the works in Jezreel together. But, on the other hand, if I kill their six champions, then Alden is returned unharmed, the six girls come home and the six other girls come back too—and there'll be no more hostages. I don't think they'll agree to or even consider surrendering Your Princess, Altara. I'm sorry I can't accomplish that, too. But if I can stop this annual tribute, it won't be so bad, will it?"

Rounder and rounder grew the Atlantean's eyes, and he

gaped like a school boy in a side show.

"What sayest thou? Thou alone to overcome six of their best warriors? Nay, but this is folly! Moonshine! What knowest thou of their weapons?"

"Nothing," admitted Nelson, "but I do know Brother Winchester here." He patted the smooth stock. "He's mighty persuasive, properly handled."

"But they are armored! They have the fungus bombs, the light retortii and the javelin!"

"Righto!" agreed Nelson a trifle carelessly, "but you don't know what this old boy can do when he's put to it. Well?"

"By Saturn!" An uncertain ring crept into the Atlantean Prince's voice. "A moment, while I address His Splendor."

"I'm a fool, a damn fool!" thought Nelson. "Still, it's Alden's only chance—unless the Jarmuthians've got some trick I'm not on to, I ought to stand a fighting chance." Meanwhile Emperor and Captain-General drew to one side, listening to Hero John's impassioned oratory. That the idea met with disapproval, Nelson quietly recognized from the incredulous, even contemptuous, glances Altorius shot at him. Leaving the four sneering Jarmuthians under guard of the nobles, the Emperor came striding impatiently over the inlaid floor.

"What madness is this?" he demanded harshly. "Dost thou realize what would hang upon thy skill? If thou shouldst fail, our annual hostage for the divine Altara would be twelve instead of six of our maidens. Further, the dog-conceived Jereboam would wax unbearably overweening and insolent. Nay, there is too much at hazard! Though outnumbered we will give battle in the morning."

"Yes?" demanded Nelson, in turn impatient. "A fine chance you'd stand! Why, less than half of your army is here at Cerium and Hero John tells me that the enemy have massed their entire forces on the salient of Poseidon. Isn't that so?"

Altorius' handsome brow darkened. "Aye," he admitted, "but our reinforcing corps will come up before the third hour of the third division."

Here Hero Giles broke in and, speaking with the quick, impassioned tones of one whose reactions are violent, pled for confidence in the American. "Nay, fair cousin," he replied, casting a sidewise look at the Jarmuthians standing in muttered colloquy with their leader, who had now gotten to his feet and was angrily dabbing the blood from his chin with the hem of his yellow kiltlike garment. "I saw with mine own eyes what miracles Friend Nelson doth perform with his curious noise-making retortii. If Jereboam falls upon us ere our regiments are marshaled, then, verily, are we doomed. We have no choice but to play for time. Harken to the counsel of Hero John! Methinks this stranger from the Ice World is no braggart. He will fight well. If he loses he dies horribly—that he knows. The thought will strengthen his arms, and if he wins—!"

Then broke in Nelson firmly. "If I win I must have the word of Your Majesty that Alden and I are to be afforded all help and free passage to that place where your soldiers captured my friend. It that understood?"

Altorius' blue eyes shifted and there was a slight hesitation in his manner. Then, coming to a decision, he whirled and extended his hand.

"Good, 'tis agreed," he said. "On my head be it. Have patience while Hero Giles confers with these outlandish dogs."

It was with intense interest that the anxious aviator watched the ensuing conference. He could see the four

Jarmuthians listening, dark eyes restlessly flitting back and forth, and their mouths twisted into contemptuous half snarls. Then, as Nelson's offer was made clear, a look of cunning seemed to creep into the eyes of the leader. He asked for clarification of several points, then, being informed of the details, his thick lips parted in an evil, crafty grin.

Taken aback at the suspiciously ready acquiescence of the enemy, Hero Giles turned about. "They agree," he translated, "that, should Friend Nelson win, they will return to their own land, they will forfeit the annual tribute forever and return the other stranger unharmed. They speak fair, but I fear—" He bit his lips in perplexity. "These dogs, who talk with the forked tongues of serpents, plan some snare, some cunning trickery."

"Repeat the terms." Altorius seemed gripped with apprehension too. "Let all be clearly understood: at the third division of morning will the wanderer fight six warriors. No more and no less."

This was agreed and reaffirmed. Then, with an insolent, triumphant laugh, the Jarmuthian delegation whirled about and stalked from the room, their dark greaved legs flashing in military unison over the polished floor.

"'Tis done," quoth Hero Giles gloomily. "The encounter will take place on the plain of Gilboa at the third hour of the third division. And may Saturn help us if thy might fails, Friend Nelson! For then surely will the hordes of Jarmuth despoil us and there will come a desolation and a darkness upon the Empire of Atlans."

CHAPTER V

It seemed incredibly soon that Victor Nelson found himself striding out from the serrated ranks of the Atlantean army which, drawn up in a rough diamond formation, looked discouragingly small in comparison to that vast sea of helmets twinkling ominously across the plain of Poseidon amid a haze of bright yellow dust which climbed lazily into the breathless heavens. The Jarmuthian army, numbering perhaps sixty or seventy thousand effective troops, lay encamped in a great salient formed by a convolution of the Apidanus and formed the only Jarmuthian tract of the great valley lying south of the boiling river.

Like low-lying snow drifts, the sheen of the enemy tents struck Nelson's eye as he strode over the bright green turf to battle for Richard Alden's life.

"There was something back of those nasty grins of the ambassadors," he reflected. "I wonder what deviltry they're cooking up?"

He glanced at a stalwart Atlantean herald who, nervous in the extreme, clutched his brazen, dolphin-shaped horn and followed in the American's wake together with a sad little company. Weeping, moaning and dressed in plain black robes marched six really lovely girls—they who would perish on Beelzebub's altar if Nelson failed. Bitter were the looks of the guards as they secured the hands of the victims and many the hopeful look cast at the impassive American when they turned back, leaving the helpless girls to their fate.

The ground where the one-sided duel was to take place was marked off by means of little yellow flags on a level plain perhaps a quarter of a mile long and wide. Arriving on the nearest border Nelson briefly motioned the herald to halt.

"Might as well start shooting at the best range possible, and beat their steam throwers," he decided. "Wish to the devil I'd a few more cartridges. Only thirteen shots between me and Beelzeebub's altar in Jezreel, so I'd better not miss. All right, son, toot your horn."

With his thumb be gestured the command, whereupon the Atlantean nodded eagerly and, filling his chest, set horn to lips to blow a long, strident note that rang harshly, boldly out over the great plain.

While the note of the challenge rang out, Nelson's eyes turned back to regard the Atlantean array and detected, far in the rear, a huge pillar of dust which must mark the progress of the Atlantean reinforcements. Would they arrive at Cierum in time? Then his eyes sought that spot where Altorius and his staff sat anxiously on their podokos, watching intently the impending struggle. Very clearly the flash of their armor came to him.

"I guess, like the girls back there, they're kind of nervous and jumpy," thought Nelson. "Well, I don't blame them. I've had quieter moments myself."

Having blown three blasts, the Atlantean herald saluted; then, with disconcerting haste, made his way back to the ranks of his fellows some two hundred yards away.

From the Jarmuthian army came an answering blast. Nelson cast a last look on the Atlantean army, breathlessly awaiting the impending duel. There was the allosauri corps on the far left; he could see the chimeric monsters' long, repulsive necks writing endlessly back and forth through the air as they squealed and tugged strongly at their restraining chains. On the right were stationed perhaps ten thousand podokesons, their slender, yellow-shafted lances swaying like a sapling forest in the distance. In the center were eleven thousand protection infantry, green-crested and armed with compact tanks of blue-maxima vapor, fungus bombs and swords. Behind them, and corresponding to heavy infantry, were ranged some twenty thousand blue-plumed hoplites, eagerly fingering the brazen hoses of their death dealing portable retortii.

Nelson had no time to further study the array, for he whirled about as from the Atlantean army arose a deep, horrified shout. He stood paralyzed, his jaw slack. For there, waddling slowly forward, came the most fantastic huge creature imaginable. Unspeakably repellent and horrible, it stood on short legs thick as mature trees, to tower at least thirty-five feet above the ground at the fore-shoulders! An immense reptilian neck some twenty-five feet long weaved continuously back and forth, while a surprisingly small, bullet-shaped head emitted rumbling grunts.

"Great God!" gasped the horrified aviator, and felt the ground sway under him. "It must be ninety feet long!"

Paralyzed by a dreadful fascination he watched the ungainly, hill-like reptile shuffle ponderously forward and realized that, high on its back, was fixed a small fort, rather like those howdahs or boxes which are fastened to the backs of elephants. Chilled with the nearness of death, Nelson counted six mail-clad warriors in the howdah. Then the true import of the Jarmuthians evil jest struck him with full force.

"Six men, they said. And six men there are—but the treacherous devils mounted them on that walking hill-side! Guess Altorius can kiss his six girls good-by right now. Poor Alden! Well, I did my best—a rotten trick."

At that moment he felt as an ant must feel on beholding the approach of a human. It was terrifying, the inexorable advance of that colossal, fantastic monster. From behind he could hear the infuriated shouts of the Atlantean army. They knew even he could not hope to withstand the murderous onslaught of the beast now entering the duelling space.

On came the diplodocus, its vast warty tail trailing over the ground and raising a heavy column of dust, while its mud smeared sides bore out Hero Giles' statement that here was one of those semi-aquatic titans from the steaming swamps of Jarmuth.

"Hell! Poor Alden's as good as finished now! What a fool I was to think I could save him!"

Obedient to an overwhelming fear, Nelson whirled to flee, then stopped, as, from the depths of his being, a stronger power forbade him to desert his friend to certain death.

"Range two hundred and fifty yards," he estimated, and, whipping up the Winchester, sighted full at the ponderous creature's slimy snakelike head. When the recoil jarred his shoulder, Nelson dropped the barrel an inch or so to watch. Nothing happened. The great beast was advancing as before, its incredibly long neck weaving steadily back and forth as though to sniff the air.

"Hell!"

Struck by a sudden thought, he snatched a cartridge from his pocket and, with that strength which comes to men in their hour of mortal peril, wrenched out the metal-jacketed bullet, to reinsert it backwards into the brass cartridge case.

Meanwhile the vast brute had drawn nearer, crushing flat a young oak in its path as easily as though it had been a wheat stalk.

"Maybe this dum-dum will do some good," panted Nelson. "If it doesn't, nothing will stop it!"

Again he sighted until, finding those small, orange red

eyes in line with his sight, he fired. This time the gray-brown monster uttered a titanic bellow of rage, halted, and began shaking its clumsy blunt head.

"Hit it, by God!" exulted Nelson, and seized the momentary respite to slip two fresh cartridges into the Winchester's magazine.

But, to his inexpressible dismay, the monster presently resumed its ponderous progress while the Jarmuthians in the howdah uttered taunting yells that reached him faintly, while the sun flares glinted on their brandished swords and lances. One of them plucked a fungus grenade from his belt and flung it with all his might in Nelson's direction. The missile fell to the earth far short of its destination and seemed to break rather than explode, at the same time expelling that deadly, greenish-yellow vapor which, blown away by a strong wind, fortunately came nowhere near the doomed aviator.

"Oh! You will?"

Nelson sighted swiftly at the grenade-thrower and fired, whereupon the Jarmuthian, some hundred and fifty yards distant, spun crazily about, flung both arms towards the amber-yellow sky and toppled from the howdah, for all the world like a diver in quest of pearls.

From both breathless armies rose a terrific shout. Accustomed as they were to the visible destruction of the retortii, this noisy yet invisible death was appalling.

But Nelson's agonized attention was not on the assembled armies, for nearer came the mountainous diplodocus, its lumbering strides making the howdah sway like a ship in a gale and preventing use of the portable retortii.

Nelson planted both feet, took fresh grip on his waning courage and shot again, this time aiming at a gigantic, black bearded warrior who seemed to be training one of those portable retortii upon him.

Again the Winchester cracked and this time the black bearded man sank from sight back into the howdah, while his companions, uttering vengeful shouts, tossed more fungus bombs at the lone heroic figure barring their progress towards the six bound and shrieking maidens.

Towering thrice as high as the largest African elephant, the diplodocus was now but seventy-five yards away. He had hit it, that Nelson could tell, for a large shower of blood sprayed from the monster's neck. Then, uttering a despairing curse, he sent a shot smacking squarely into the left shoulder, at the base of that mastlike neck with fervent hope of finding the heart. But the heavy bullet bothered the cyclopean reptile no more than a sting of a mosquito.

On, on it came. In another minute it must stamp out Victor Nelson's life beneath feet as large as hogsheads.

"Damn!"

Nelson snapped the ejector lever, throwing out the spent cartridge.

"No use," he whispered, "can't faze that hill of meat! But I might as well kill all of those bloody cannibals I can."

With amazing speed and accuracy he picked off two of the remaining Jarmuthians, whose shining, bronze armor could nowise withstand the wicked impact of modern nickel-jacketed bullets. One of the stricken men for a moment dangled with the last of his strength from one of the chains securing the howdah to the enormous creature's back, then tumbled heavily some forty feet to the earth.

Only two shots more in the magazine—! Nelson suddenly found himself very cool. "Two shots and then—"

He was conscious of that great, snakelike head darting viciously in his direction. A huge, slobbering mouth, studded with teeth a foot long, yawned redly before him like a nightmare incarnate, blotting out consciousness of all else. Then Victor Nelson, fighting to control his strumming nerves, deliberately sighted into a great, orange colored eye, saw the narrow black iris over the Winchester's front sight and knew the huge warty head was not ten feet away.

He pressed the trigger and never heard the report, but felt the blast of a furnace-hot breath in his face—a breath that stank like the foul reek of burning rubber.

With a detached sense of surprise he saw the eye miraculously and dreadfully disintegrate; then, as the bitter smell of burned cordite stung his nostrils, he sprang violently sidewise to find himself staring up at the howdah, now towering at least forty feet above.

The next few moments were indescribable. Horrible roars and bellows, loud as those of a thousand angered bulls, shattered the air. The diplodocus halted, stunned by pain and the partial loss of eyesight; then, its infinitesimal brain becoming gripped with fear, it plunged and lumbered sidewise, nearly shaking the warriors from the howdah, where they clung for dear life. Nelson was barely able to avoid the sweep of the powerful tail as the diplodocus wheeled about on hind legs, reeled and started blindly back towards the Jarmuthian ranks. Suddenly it stood stock still, shaking with super-elephantine motions. Then, for all the world like a balky mule, it sank to the earth and cowered there, despite the frantic efforts of the surviving Jarmuthians to stir it to obedience.

By the strong amber light of the sun flare Nelson had a vision of the last two warriors swinging in apelike agility to the ground. They were giants, those two men of Jarmuth, and their conical helmets added additional stature. One of them, shouting an unintelligible taunt, reached for his belt to snatch out a fungus bomb, but Nelson, dropping on one knee, sent a bullet crashing between the Jarmuthian's scowling eyes. Even as he fell, the last of the six champions unwisely ignored his retortii and frantically sprang forward, razor-edged sword upraised.

Nelson frantically worked the ejector lever but only an empty click resulted! His heart sank. "Hell! the magazine's empty!"

He had just time to swing the Winchester about and grasp its barrel as the Jarmuthian, with a loud shout, sprang in, slashing viciously at Nelson's unprotected neck. Using the clubbed rifle like a baseball bat, the American struck out with the strength of despair. There came a resonant clang as blade and barrel encountered each other. Steel is ever stronger than bronze, so Nelson had the satisfaction of seeing the Jarmuthian's sword blade break squarely in two near the hilt.

Horrified, the black bearded warrior glanced at the empty hilt in his hand but, courageous to the end, sprang in like a tiger to grapple with that small, agile man in khaki and serge.

"You would—eh?" gasped Nelson.

Putting all his strength behind a blow he whirled up the heavy Winchester, struck out and felt the solid walnut stock smash fair and square on the conical helmet. Like an eggshell the bronze helm broke and the six-pointed star above went spinning off into the dust. As a tree sways before it falls beneath a forester's ax, so the dark Jarmuthian giant tottered, while the wide dusty plain of Poseidon echoed with a rumbling, incredulous shout.

"There," choked Nelson, incredulous to be still alive, "I guess that'll be about all for today."

But he was wrong. From the ranks of Jarmuth rose a terrible, ominous cry and at the same time there broke out the sibilant hiss of a thousand retortii. From the Atlantean army came an answering yell and Nelson turned to race back to the shelter of Altorius' body-guard, pausing but to arouse the terrified hostages. Swiftly he cast loose their bonds and pointed to the nearest detachment of Atlanteans. Sobbing with joy the six girls fled for dear life just as the first of the allosauri went racing over the plains. Screaming, all-powerful and uncanny war dogs, they bounded grotesquely high in the air, plunging straight towards the Jarmuthian ranks which greeted them with a searing, billowing blast of their retortii. Though dozens of the terrible creatures fell kicking and writhing beneath the scalding discharge of the retortii, the main body, perhaps forty or fifty in number, sprang like rending fiends into the dense packed masses of Jarmuthian infantry.

Of the ensuing battle, Nelson had but the most confused recollections. The dominating impression was that the fray was awesome, horrible beyond power of description. He recalled feeding the five remaining cartridges into the magazine, then clapping on an Atlantean noble's helmet. With Hero John at his side he joined in an furious headlong charge of the podoko corps.

Like a vast glittering wedge the gallant Atlantean lancers advanced under shelter of the blue maxima vapor which, discharged by the protectons or light infantry, dispelled the scalding steam clouds launched from the Jarmuthian portable retortii.

"Halor vàn!" Hero John shouted the Atlantean war cry. "Halor vàn! Come Friend Nelson, this day shall the treacherous swine of Jarmuth drown in their own blood! Halor vàn!"

Nelson replied nothing. He was too busy drawing a bead on a gorgeously arrayed enemy officer who appeared to be directing the defence.

Faster and faster rushed the podokos, forty, fifty miles an hour, a carnate thunderbolt hurled straight at the enemy center. Under a hot fire of grenades dozens of the lancers fell and once, when a fungus bomb broke near by, Nelson saw half a dozen Atlanteans tumble from their saddles, the hideous yellow growths already sprouting from nostrils, mouth and ears. The turmoil became deafening, indescribable—like the roar of a crowded subway.

The American had a brief glimpse of a mountainous diplodocus assailed by half a dozen hissing, shrieking allosauri who, employing jaws and claws, ripped great, shuddering chucks of flesh from the agonized and unwieldy monster on whose back the frantic Jarmuthians fought with terrible ferocity.

As agile as grasshoppers, those fierce war dogs ripped and worried their prey. One of them clung like a bulldog to the doomed diplodocus' head, though the twenty-foot neck writhed and whirled frantically in effort to shake it loose. Another allosaurus, whining with eagerness, actually clambered up the back of an assailed giant only to fall back under the blast of a retortii mounted in the howdah. Bathed in live steam, with bones showing through its melting, quivering flesh, the allosaurus collapsed backwards, but another instantly took its place and, gaining its goal with a terrific leap, made a shambles of the howdah, tearing the men in it apart as a lion does an antelope.

Nelson found himself very busy. The charging podokesos were now in the midst of the Jarmuthian heavy infantry, slashing down at a maze of yelling, black-bearded, Semitic faces. Once Nelson was nearly speared, shooting his assailant just as the lance glimmered over his heart. Again he saw the Atlantean hoplites beaten back amid a pestilential fog of fungus gas which stretched them in kicking, loathsome heaps on the dusty plain. The uproar became terrific, indescribable, as the whistling screams of the allosauri and the saurean bellows of the diplodoci rose above the shouts of the soldiery to fill the dust-laden air with a dreadful clamor. The battle now swayed critically; a feather's weight on either side and one army would roll back in red, irretrievable ruin. It was the psychological instant. Nelson sensed it unerringly.

"Look!" shouted Hero John, dashing a rivulet of blood from his eyes, "there fights the dog-begotten Jereboam himself! Halor vàn! Smite, ye soldiers of Atlans! Smite!"

Following the line of the outstretched hand. Nelson caught a glimpse of an enormous, eagle nosed warrior who, clad in gleaming, diamond studded harness, fought like a paladin of old. Powerful as a dark Ares the sable browed Jereboam raged among the dismayed Atlantean hoplites, beating them to earth with terrible ferocity.

It was a long shot, one he might readily have been forgiven in missing but with the speed of thought Victor Nelson sprang from his podoko, dropped on one knee behind a pile of corpses and, uttering a fervent prayer, fired full at Jereboam's black head.

The nearest combatants drew back momentarily at the unfamiliar thunder of the report and fell silent while the groans and shrieks of the wounded rose loud. As a man looking through many thickness of glass, so Nelson saw Jereboam reel on his splendidly caparisoned podoko, clasp both hands to his forehead and sink to earth.

Hero Giles, somewhere far in the Atlantean van, saw what transpired and capitalized it with the inspiration of a genius.

"Jereboam is dead!" he shouted in ringing tones, and flashed his red stained sword. "Woe to Jarmuth this day! Smite, ye sons of Atlans. Woe to Jarmuth—Jereboam is fallen!"

And smite hard the reinforced Atlanteans did. Filled with a new courage they advanced so determinedly that the disconcerted and dismayed Jarmuthians broke and fled in a disastrous, panic-stricken rout back over the plain of Poseidon towards the boiling river.

The ground was already carpeted with dead and with abandoned equipment, when fresh packs of allosauri were loosed on the fleeing Jarmuthians to wreak havoc indescribable and, ere long, only the triumphant, panting Atlanteans remained on the field.

CHAPTER VI

There was music and high revelry in the fortress of Cierum that night, and Victor Nelson, embarrassed and flushed with the extravagant adoration of all Atlans, sat by the Emperor Altorius' side waiting, watching for the appearance of a humbled Jarmuthian delegation.

"Never since the world began has there been such a hero in Atlans!" cried Altorius, his face more Roman than ever. "Prithee tarry amongst us, Hero Nelson. Thou shalt be as my brother. A marble palace shalt thou have and twenty wives, each fair as those damsels which thou hast, by thy might, rescued from the profane altar of the fiend, Beelzebub!"

"Thanks," laughed Nelson, and drained a goblet of tawny wine. "I'd be delighted to stay, but the point is—He broke off short, for there came a sudden tramp of feet at the door of the great hall and there, just visible above the green crests of the royal guards, he recognized that pale, drawn face which had haunted him ever since he had returned to find the abandoned aeroplane.

"Dick!" he shouted. "Dick Alden!"

"Nelson!"

With that same irresistible form which had won a certain November classic for Harvard, Richard Alden bucked and plunged through a double rank of startled guards and came running across the marble floor, his eyes lit with an unspeakable gladness.

"Nelson! Nelson!" he panted. "What in hell are you doing up there?"

"Oh!" replied the aviator with a joyous grin, "just visiting with my friend, the Emperor."

Alden halted, on his handsome features a curious mixture of surprise and delight. "The Emperor?" he stammered. "You sitting beside an Emperor?"

"Would it not seem so?" inquired Altorius with a low laugh.

"It would," chuckled Alden. "Victor Nelson, as I remember, always was a good politician."

"And," thought Nelson, "I'll have to be a damn sight better one to get us out of Atlans without injuring Altorius' feelings. I don't suppose he'll ever be able to realize that all the desirable things in the world don't lie in this valley."

Throngs of brilliantly armored and plumed officers and courtiers, some of them nursing wounds and bandaged heads, came up to hail the mighty wanderer who had subdued the might of Jarmuth.

Flushed and pleased, as is any normal man under well-earned praise, Nelson shook one wiry fist after another, while Alden chatted with the Emperor. Nobles, officers and courtiers all pressed close to fawn upon the new hero— but, far back in the council chamber, a group of dark robed priests were crowded together. Haranguing the priests was a fierce, white bearded old man who seemed to be arguing violently.

"Hum!" thought the American. "That's at least one outfit that doesn't like the way I part my hair. Wonder what devilment the priests are cooking up?"

He was not long in finding out, for the black robed arch-priest suddenly left his group of underlings to boldly make his way forward, while princes, courtiers and warriors drew respectfully aside and bent their heads.

"Hail! All conquering Emperor!" The stern old man

halted squarely before Altorius' gem encrusted throne, while Alden checked some remark to look curiously down upon the hawk-featured arch-priest.

Altorius flushed and the lines about his mouth tightened, from which Nelson guessed that there was more than a little bad blood between the spiritual and temporal heads of the empire.

"What wouldst thou, oh Heracles?"

"I would know why the all powerful Wanderer, of whom thou makest so much, did not rescue Princess Altara?"

The Emperor stiffened. "Her rescue, being impossible of accomplishment, was not nominated in the agreement," he said coldly. "The Wanderer has in full carried out his share—and so shall we. Honored and beloved of Atlans, these great warriors shall abide among us in peace."

Here Nelson thought it wise to dispel any illusions Altorius might entertain about their staying in Atlans. "No, oh Splendor: remember, our agreement was that, should I conquer the Jarmuthian champions, Alden and I were to be allowed to go free."

"Nay, oh Splendor," fiercely broke in the arch-priest, "permit them not to go. I tell thee the Princess Altara *must* be restored to Atlans! Else—" a distinct note of threat crept into the old man's voice. "—else evil days shall fall upon this empire, and the line of Hudson will wither and fade."

Up sprang Altorius in a towering rage. "Sirrah! Dost dare make threats to thy liege lord?"

Fire flashed from the young Emperor's bright blue eyes, and under their fierce glare the old man quailed and stepped back with eyes lowered.

"Altorius keeps his word," the Emperor thundered. "The strangers shall go, though all the black-robed kites in the realm say me nay. The word of a Hudsonian prince is as sure as the fire of Pelion. Get thee gone, rash priest!"

A long moment, the two strangely contracting figures glared at each other, the young, splendid Emperor and the malevolent, withered old man.

"The Gods demand their daughter," cried Heracles in parting, "and woe to him who says them nay!"

With this parting shot, the arch-priest turned and, scarlet faced, stalked from the council room, while Altorius threw back his head and roared with laughter.

"Come, oh ye Heroes, ye princes and captains! Come, let us make festival before these mighty wanderers go their way!"

Roar upon roar of enthusiasm echoed through the marble throne room, and Nelson would have felt wholly at ease had not that little knot of priests remained gathered like ill-omened carrion crows about the door. Muttering among themselves, they were watching him with a curious intentness that aroused deep misgivings in the American's mind, and it was with something like a sigh that he joined the procession forming to proceed to the triumphal feast on which the wealth and luxury of the whole empire of Atlans had been lavished.

CHAPTER VII

"That's one of the fixed retortiis I was speaking about," remarked Victor Nelson as he paused to point out a tapering brass tube which was mounted on a platform above the long staircase up which he and Alden were toiling. "It's a big brute: see how small the gunners look beside it? These steam guns are wonderful things."

The younger aviator sighed. "I've had enough of miracles," he said wiping his flushed features and hitching a small pack higher on his leather-clad shoulders. "All I want to do is to lay my weary eyes on the plane again. What with these ghastly allosauri, diplodocuses and other monsters, I'm damn well fed up with this place."

Nelson settled his Winchester rifle more comfortably into the hollow of his arm. "Correct. So am I. But we can't say Altorius didn't do right by our Nell. Good Lord, what a triumph he gave us!" The dark pilot's smile flashed from beneath his neat, close-clipped black mustache. "Wait till Cartier gets a peep at those diamonds he gave us."

Panting, the two halted by mutual consent. "Ever see so many stairs?" grunted Nelson. "Three more flights and we'll be into the tunnel; ah, there's the opening. I only hope these blighters haven't hurt the plane."

Before resuming the climb Nelson shifted his rifle, idly regarding the armored gunners just above; then suddenly he stiffened his wiry body with a sharp cry. "Look out, Dick! What the devil? Those damn fools ahead are swinging the retortii across our—"

The dark haired aviator's words were drowned out in a deafening, hissing roar that burst from the great retortii's throat, and his heart gave a great convulsive leap at the sight. Was this an accident—or treachery? An accident of course. Somehow he could not bring himself to think that Altorius would break his pledged word. Projected in a shimmering white arm the scalding death vapor shot across the staircase, its hot breath licking the faces of the startled and angry Americans, and quickly forcing them to turn and run downwards to avoid being scalded.

"What the devil are these idiots trying to do?" gasped Nelson, anxiously eyeing the red-crested warriors who, peering down through the blue lenses of their helmets, watched the khaki-clad aviators but made no effort to realign their retortii. "Hero Giles'll skin those fools alive if he hears of this. Guess we'd better wait a minute: they'll soon shut off the steam."

Shielding his face from the steam clouds that obliterated all view of the staircase above, Alden stood watching the billowing steam clouds in silent awe.

"Terrible, aren't they, Vic?" he remarked. "I've never seen those big fellows in action. They make the portable variety look like water pistols."

As the steam barrier showed no signs of abating, an uneasy gleam crept into Nelson's dark eye, and with jaw grimly set, he cocked the Winchester and turned with the intention of lodging a complaint at the next station below; but, to his utter dismay, he beheld bronze armored figures on the next platform now training their long-muzzled steam gun across the stair. Even as he sprang back, the deadly white vapor hissed forth from the second retortii, completely barring further retreat down the stair. Like an icy flood the chill of impending doom invaded Nelson's soul. This was no accidental discharge, for with the slightest change of direction in the deflection of either retortii, death would descend upon him and his companion.

Swiftly speech became impossible, as the roar of the huge retortii was deafening; the two were lost in the heart of an opaque cloud which completely blotted out the copper-hued Atlantean sky. Hot blood surged into Nelson's head while he became aware of ghostly and stealthy figures advancing through the shimmering billows of vapor. Up, up, they came, like dream men, their eyes weird and unreal. Cursing the treachery of their late host, Nelson and Alden watched dozens upon dozens of hoplites come swarming up the stairs in solid, dully-gleaming ranks. Apparently intent to take them prisoners, the foremost Atlanteans made a rush, giving the American time to fire just twice.

Unable to retreat, the helpless aviators stood to meet the engulfing wave of hoplites. Nelson struck out as hard as he could at those yelling, red-bearded faces, though he knew the effort was hopeless. He was dimly conscious that Alden, not far away, also fought with the vigor of despair.

With a sense of savage satisfaction, the dark haired aviator felt his fist impact solidly into a yelling, sweating face; then something struck his head and, amid a miniature sunburst, his senseless form sank limply on the damp stones of the great staircase.

After an interval, the length of which he did not know, Victor Nelson opened his eyes slowly, for his head throbbed like a savage's war drum. Uttering a stifled groan he shut the lids to still an overpowering sense of nausea which gripped him, but a moment later he made another attempt to discover in what sort of place he found himself. Gradually, his eyes became accustomed to a curious orange-red glare beyond a series of bars. Bars? The idea fixed itself in his benumbed brain; bars meant prison! Yes, those grim blank walls bore out the assumption. He lay on the damp stone floor of what must be a fairly spacious cell. Beneath his leather aviator's jacket he shuddered. "Jail, eh? What a nice place to wake up in!"

A groan from behind him prompted Nelson to painfully raise his head and look about. He blinked dazedly, meanwhile trying to focus his eyes, then he heaved a faint sigh of relief as his gaze encountered the muscular, well-proportioned figure of Richard Alden, who half sat, half reclined, against one of the grey stone walls, burying a ghastly pale face between trembling hands.

"You hurt?" To speak, Nelson drew a slightly deeper breath and at once became conscious of a horrible, throat-wrenching stench. Dimly, he recalled having once before encountered such an odor; when was it? Oh, yes; during the Great War when he'd stumbled into a dugout tenanted by long unburied corpses. A cold finger stabbed at his brain. Corpses.

"Are you hurt, Dick?" he repeated hoarsely.

The lax figure stirred and Alden's blonde head was raised slowly. "I don't know." His voice came very thickly. "I—I'm still dizzy. What's happened?"

"Damned if I know; but those bright boys have evidently heaved us into a calaboose of some kind!"

Nelson, on peering about, had discovered that one end of the cell was closed only by a series of massive bronze bars; the two other walls were solid masonry; while the fourth was also solid but fitted with a small oval door of bronze.

"Calaboose? The hell you say!" Alden coughed feebly. "My God, but that steam was terrible stuff. I nearly smothered before I got knocked out."

Slowly, the younger aviator looked about, and suddenly his eyes widened in an expression of indescribable horror.

"Look!" Alden's voice had died to a shaken whisper. "My God, Nelson, we're finished! Look at that allosaurus!"

Following the line indicated by the pilot's shaking fore-finger, Nelson peered out through the series of great bars while a shudder shook his aching body. Though he had seen these fearful monsters on many occasions, yet it was never from such a position as that in which he now found himself. To his ears came a sibilant hissing like that of a thousand serpents; and, quivering in every nerve, he forced his eyes open once again, to discover that the cell which he and his companion occupied was but one of a series of cells surrounding a huge square in which were imprisoned perhaps twenty or thirty of those horrible, gargoylesque creatures which were the Atlantean dogs of war. Some thirty-four feet in length, the enormous, slate-grey monsters hopped leisurely about, their warty hides and huge luminous eyes betraying their reptilian origin. In shape the allosauri resembled loathsome and titanic kangaroos as they lumbered awkwardly to and fro, picking viciously at what appeared to be fragments of human flesh and bones.

While the two prisoners crouched paralyzed with horror, one of the nightmarish creatures came hopping over and, pressing a head as big as a steam scoop against the bars, stared in with huge, pale green eyes. A long minute the ghastly creature remained looking in, clearly outlined by the orange glow from outside.

The doomed aviators found something fearfully fascinating about those narrow vertical irises set in pupils the size of dinner plates. Uttering a deep growl, the allosaurus shuffled nearer, and impatiently rubbed its huge, bullet head against the bars; then gripped the ponderous bronze bars with its ridiculously small front legs to shake the whole grille-work with a savagery that dislocated bits of plaster and made the metal reverberate. While Nelson and Alden shrank flat against the far wall, a scarlet tongue at least four feet long flicked the air but a few feet from their bloodless, sweating visages. Becoming irritated at the sturdiness of the barrier, the mountainous reptile tugged harder and hissed, filling the cell with a foul exhalation that stank like the reeks of smoldering rags.

Nelson's wavering consciousness reeled, and a mad, dreadful fear, like that a dreamer suffers in the grip of nightmare, invaded his being. He felt the hairs rising on the nape of his neck.

But, with a squall of rage, the monster abandoned its futile efforts and leaped away. Feigning indifference, the allosaurus picked up a half-gnawed skull with its tiny forelegs; and, while the prisoners watched, it stuffed the head into a maw twice the size of an elephant's and crunched the gruesome tidbit as easily as a boy would a walnut. Presently it shuffled off to rejoin the hideous herd in the center of the court.

"Nice kind of a jail we've been thrown into. Wish I could understand what's happened." Alden buried his face in his hands. "It kind of looks as though Altorius had a change of heart."

Nelson replied nothing, but sat staring fixedly out into the horrible court.

"Somehow, I don't think Altorius would do such a thing," he said at last. "Let's think back and see if we can't piece this treachery together."

"Wish I had your faith in the Emperor—but I haven't." Alden's handsome face twisted itself into a wry smile.

"Let's see, now," persisted Nelson, fingering a square jaw upon which sprouted a thick growth of reddish bristles. "There was a deputation of priests to see Altorius yesterday. They were clamoring for the return of Altara—the Sacred Virgin—and looked pretty mad when he put them off."

"Maybe this is the private doing of the priests," admitted Alden. "Anyway, we're in one devil of a fix. There's certainly no way out of this calaboose—and those damned brutes out there look hungry."

Nelson frowned, deep in thought. "Wish I could find a reasonable explanation. I really don't think it's Altorius; still, that's what you get for mixing in on the politics of these forgotten kingdoms."

"But," reminded the other, "you had no choice, old lad. Remember, you mixed in to save me."

From across the courtyard rang a loud, penetrating shriek of fear that made the two aviators spring to their feet and rush to the bars. Peering across the court, they discovered three naked men shrieking and clinging frantically to the bars of an exactly similar cell.

"What's wrong with them?" demanded Alden as the agonized screams rang louder still.

"I don't know," was Alden's breathless reply. "But what's that noise?"

A curious metallic clanking sound filled the poisoned air, and for a moment Nelson remained utterly puzzled. Then, as the noise grew louder, the allosauri commenced to betray a strange restlessness. They ceased basking and feeding, and their hideous heads commenced to dart quickly this way and that.

* * * * *

While the terrific shrieks of the wretches across the court rang to the copper-hued sky, the two Americans remained in doubt; then all at once the chill of death gripped their hearts, as they saw the bars of that cell directly opposite slowly but surely rising! Uttering heart-rending cries, the doomed prisoners clung frantically to stay the vanishing barrier separating them from those appalling man-eaters. But, disdainful of their pitiful efforts, the bronze bars rose relentlessly with metallic rattlings and janglings from some unseen mechanism.

Rooted to the floor, both Americans watched the distant grille vanish into the upper stone-work and heard the ghastly hissing as the allosauri herd commenced to move forward. Sick and shaken, Nelson beheld one of the doomed men cling in desperation to the bars; he was lifted clear of the floor and borne towards the ceiling, meanwhile venting his terror with such screams as could otherwise have risen only from an inquisitor's torture chamber.

The tragedy was swiftly completed. Half a dozen of the nearest allosauri, taller than any giraffes, suddenly sprang forward, their long, naked tails rising as their gait increased. Snarling horribly, the vast slate-colored beasts plunged into the cell, terminating shrieks of mortal terror. Backs broader than bus tops squirmed and tugged, then one of the loathsome monsters reappeared carrying in its dripping jaws a mangled, yet struggling victim much as a cat carries a mouse. In a trice the other allosauri came rushing eagerly up, seeking to snatch the prey from the first monster.

Nelson stiffened. "Great God! And that's what'll happen to us!"

Weakened by his head wound, and blind with nausea, he stumbled to the rear of the cell to collapse upon a pile of foul straw, littered with equipment which the superstitious captors must have condemned together with the owners.

Nelson sank upon them, then stiffened, for his outflung hand had encountered a hard, familiar outline. It was a .45 automatic pistol.

A moment's furious search revealed that the captors had missed or not understood the use of the weapon in Alden's leather flying coat.

"God, but we're lucky," Nelson panted. "The Atlanteans never saw this pistol of yours. They're only used to my rifle."

Hope lit Alden's features, then faded. "But what good is a .45 against brutes like those? Might at well have a pop gun!"

"Still we're lucky," grunted Nelson, delighted to find the magazine yet filled. "Can't tell what's ahead. Yes, we're the luckiest—"

He broke off in quick alarm. From overhead had come a premonitory clang! Somewhere a tackle whined and, with a sense of suffocation, both men realised that now the bars of *their* prison were beginning to creep up into a long slit in the stone ceiling!

Cold fingers of fear clutched Nelson's heart as the terrible allosauri, their jaws yet dripping redly, wheeled about at the familiar sound—to stand listening. Up and up crept the ponderous grille, while the allosauri commenced to shuffle forward, fixing on their next victims enormous, unblinking green eyes.

While the whole loathsome cell spun about, Victor Nelson forced stiff fingers to throw off the safety catch as the nearest allosaurus opened its cavernous mouth in anticipation, displaying an array of curved teeth, as long and sharp as bayonets. Standing some fifteen feet high at the shoulder the horrible creature's body was; it all but blotted out the light. The bars rose inexorably. Now they were waist high.... Now above Nelson's head.... In a moment would come the rush.

Richard Alden stood up straight and squared his shoulders. "Good-by, Vic," he said, in clear, unafraid tones. "I don't imagine that .45 will even tickle those ghastly brutes."

Nelson nodded. "All over but the cheering," he replied with that strange, macabre humor which often comes to solace men about to die.

"See you in church." There was an equally gallant lightness to Alden's reply.

The dark haired pilot, with a curious, detached sense of unreality, stepped into the middle of the room, the automatic in his hand seeming no more potent than a water pistol, for a ponderous, lambent eyed monster was now hopping forward. While minute particles of dust and dirt rained down from the disappearing barrier, the foremost allosaurus opened its enormous jaws, uttered an eery scream and charged straight at the unbarred cell.

Drawing a deep breath, Nelson raised the .45, sighted, and, remembering his former experience, fired at the enormous right eye. As in a dream, he felt the recoil. The monster neither slowed nor swerved in the least, though its great, saucer-like eye disintegrated horribly. Immediately Nelson swiftly sighted at the other eye and fired, just as the allosaurus' shadow filled the threshold.

Crack! A swirl of bitter smoke stung the aviator's staring eyes. He'd hit; he knew it!

Cyclopean moments followed as the blinded monster

dashed forward, missed the circular door, and, butting his head against the stone wall to the left, fell completely stunned, effectively blocking the doorway with its huge body. One enormous hind leg, fully ten feet long, and equipped with three razor-like claws, projected into the cell and lashed aimlessly back and forth, forcing the two prisoners to dodge wildly.

There ensued that indescribable kind of a moment when men go mad. Outside the cell the ravenous herd pounced upon their fallen mate and with hideous grunts and snarls promptly commenced to tear it apart. The shaken prisoners realized that the rending jaws would before long undoubtedly remove the temporary obstacle; but meanwhile the hideous hissing and the fetid stench of the allosauri breath made the cell a mad-house.

Gradually, the gigantic carcass at the door commenced to quiver and roll violently under the ferocious tugs of the eager feasters. A gap of light appeared over the huge haunches, and, all at once, another of those terrible heads slipped over the carcass and into the cell.

Again the .45 thundered, lighting the darkened cell with a brief orange flame. A noise like the furious trumpeting of a dozen elephants nearly blew Nelson flat as the wounded monster drew back its head, but the respite promised to be short, for the other reptiles only re-doubled their horrid, cannibalistic rending of the carcass. When the barrier was removed there would be a general rush which the shaken aviators could not hope to stay.

Suddenly, Alden uttered a low shout and pointed to the small, oval door which had, up to this point, remained securely bolted and shut. It was swinging gradually open, rimmed with a strong reddish light.

Wide-eyed, and with black hair streaming lank over his forehead, Nelson, in the act of reloading, swung about to meet this new menace. Hell! What point was there in prolonging the pitiful struggle? What was happening?

Slowly, the door swung back, and a rosy glow lit the opening, a glow that became as strong as the gleam of a spotlight. Then, slowly, a glittering, green-crested helmet of highly polished bronze appeared, and, under it, Hero Giles' familiar features, now distorted by a terrible fear. The blue eyes seemed enormous. "Quickly!" he called. "Quick or ye are lost!"

Unbelieving of the reprieve, both the aviators stared an instant at that martial figure clad in brazen armor liberally studded with enormous diamonds and emeralds, then leaped forward with the speed of desperation, for from behind came a fierce squalling from the allosauri. As he darted towards the door Nelson had a glimpse of the carcass blocking the door commencing to slip sidewise.

Alden was already out and Nelson sped through the door barely in time to escape the razor-sharp talons of the foremost allosaurus as it scrambled into the deserted cell with a resounding bellow of disappointed fury.

CHAPTER VIII

As the door clanged shut, drowning out the allosauri's furious screams, both aviators, shaken to the depths of their beings, could do nothing but stare about them in surprise. Completely surrounding and protecting the exit stood a double rank of hoplites in bronze armor. Like unreal automata, they remained utterly motionless, fixed in the various postures of an ancient Macedonian phalanx, their broad backs gleaming dully in the light of the neon flares. As in a dream, Nelson recognized on top of each spearsman's casque the graceful Atlantean military crest—a metal dolphin from the back of which sprouted a series of bright blue feathers, arranged like a dorsal fin.

"Thank Poseidon, ye still live!" cried Hero Giles, gripping their hands eagerly. "I had fear for ye, oh my friends."

Nelson grinned. "You cut the rescue act pretty fine, but of course we're damned grateful. And now,"—eagerly seizing the Hero's splendidly muscled arm—"in God's name tell us what's happened. Why we were arrested and—nearly made into allosaurus fodder?"

Hero Giles turned from snapping an order to a subaltern who was peering down a great, shadowy hallway with a distinctly uneasy manner.

"Much," he said. "Scarcely had ye two departed from Heliopolis than the priests, mad with rage over Altara's continued captivity, dared to seize the person of His Splendor and proclaim a regency. Herakles, the arch-priest is—"

From far down the gloomy, vaulted corridor came a faint sound, rather like the distant cheering of a crowd. The hoplites, standing about, turned their helmeted heads and stared uneasily, their brazen armor glowing dully with each movement.

"I'll tell ye more later, but now—" Hero Giles' voice took on a ringing quality like the clash of steel—"there is work to be done. To rescue ye, oh Hero Nelson, I slew the guards at the lower gate, for this prison lies in the hands of a caitiff rogue, Hero Edmund, one who clings to the priestly party. We had best be off lest we be trapped and slaughtered like rats in a pit."

Very distinctly to the ears of the aviator now came the dull clash of equipment and the tread of feet.

"Forward! We must hasten to reach the podokos waiting below," cried Hero Giles, settling his ponderous helmet more squarely on his leonine head.

At once the escort of fifteen-odd hoplites commenced to move down the corridor to the left, their hands tightly gripping the butts of their retortii pistols. At their head ran Hero Giles, and by his side Alden and Victor Nelson, who gripped his .45 vowing never again to return to that ghastly cell.

A long ringing cry from the rear brought home the dread realization that the enemy had appeared. Looking back, Nelson could see the far end of the great corridor filled with menacing figures. Then his heart leaped like a deer in a thicket, for *from ahead* sounded the clash of weapons! The rescue party's retreat was cut off!

Hero Giles acted with the speed of a veteran accustomed to emergencies. "Forward!" he roared, making the bare walls reverberate and rumble with his voice. *"Halor vàn! Ula Storr!"*[1]

As by magic, there appeared before the retreating force a double rank of blue-crested hoplites who debouched

---

1   Make ready for your retortii.

from a side passage into the hall and clawed desperately for fungus bombs and retortii. Evidently they had not expected to come upon the invaders so abruptly.

"*Storr!*" Like a brazen trumpet's call, the voice of Hero Giles rang out the order to fire—which was instantly drowned out in the furious hissing of the retortii of his followers.

Ever watchful, Nelson fired at a gigantic officer who, avoiding the first steam jets, flung back his arms to hurl one of the deadly fungus bombs among the rescuers. Shattering the bronze helmet, the American's bullet struck the Atlantean squarely between the eyes, but nevertheless the stricken officer's grenade rolled forward and burst among the hindermost of Hero Giles' followers. Instantly, the deadly green mold flung itself upon the nearest hoplites and in a moment they crashed to the smooth granite floor, the yellowish growths already sprouting from nose, mouth and ears.

In the corridor reigned chaos, for Hero Giles' followers were now turning the full fury of their retortii upon the rank of men barring further flight. With dreadful ease, the scalding steam struck dead the opposing warriors, stripping the flesh from their bones as easily as a boy peels a banana.

Amid the swirling white clouds, Nelson had ghastly visions of yellow skulls, of steaming accoutrement, of limp heaps of disintegrating bodies; then silence fell, and, before he quite realized it, he, together with Alden and three hoplites who had survived the disastrous fungus grenade, were bounding along after Hero Giles' glittering figure as he led the way down one passage after another.

* * * * *

Louder than ever rang the fierce cry from the rear. Behind him Nelson could see dozens upon dozens of yelling pursuers, and knew that if he were to live he must run as never before.

Into a succession of spacious rooms dashed the fugitives; on through deserted armories where hundreds of bronze helmets dangled in orderly rows; and across silent barrack halls.

Closer and closer sounded the pursuing feet, spurring the runners to an even more headlong gait.

All at once a door loomed to the right; into this darted Hero Giles and after him pounded the two Americans and three hoplites. In an instant the six men set their shoulder to the ponderous bronze door and swung it to, just as the hiss of a retortii on the other side rose above the mad, blood-hungry clamor of the momentarily baffled rebels. Gasping and sweat-bathed, the fugitives paused only an instant.

"We've gained a short passage," gasped the Atlantean wrenching off his helmet and breast plate. The veins stood out in great blue cords on his forehead, for the weight of the armor could not have been inconsiderable. "Below wait our podokos."

Nelson stripped off his leather coat, following the example of the hoplites, who swiftly divested themselves of such cumbersome equipment as could readily be removed. Then, while the shouts of the thwarted pursuers swelled like a demonic chorus, and while feathers of steam crept under the great door, Hero Giles spun about and, with his short yellow hair gleaming bright, led on down another series of passages.

All at once the fugitives, now reduced by exhaustion to five, found themselves on a balcony overlooking the great valley of Atlans. Before them opened an enormous staircase and down this they dashed at top speed, infinitely relieved to be once more in the open air.

Running like hunted stags, the fugitives had descended but a third of the great staircase, when, from behind, came a sudden, menacing cry that warned Nelson that the pursuers had, after going a longer way around, come once more in sight.

"Ah! Poseidon blast the traitorous Edmund and his varlets! See?" panted Hero Giles pointing to a huge arch from beneath which was issuing a glittering column of shouting, swift running warriors at whose head dashed a splendidly-proportioned figure that must be Hero Edmund.

With the speed of the hunted, Hero Giles bounded forward, taking three and four steps at a stride, his jade green cloak snapping out behind. Down, ever downwards over the endless flight of stairs the aviators followed him until, spent and panting, the hard pressed five plunged down a final circular staircase and so gained a courtyard where waited a detachment of armored lancers whose yellow plumes and pennons shone bright in the glare of the flame suns. Staring anxiously upwards, the troopers nevertheless stood to attention in an orderly rank beside those curious Atlantean mounts called podokos.

During all his sojourn in Atlans, Nelson had never become used to the hideous and awe-inspiring podokos which closely resembled the allosauri but were only eighteen feet long. Like the other monsters, they had tremendously developed hind legs which promised the speed now so vital for escape and safety. Ready in the tooth-studded jaws of each podoko was fitted a bronze bit together with a bridle and reins; and cinched up on each creature's back was one of those curious Atlantean saddles, which was built up at the cantle to overcome the downward slope of the podokos' spines.

Need for vital haste was but too obvious and, as he drew near, Hero Giles gasped the command to be off.

"Quick," he shouted, his scarred visage flushed and sweat-bathed. "Saddles! Speed! Speed! Cling fast as your beasts arise!"

All five literally hurled themselves into gorgeously caparisoned saddles. Instantly, the urging squatting podokos leaped to their feet.

It was the work of a moment for Nelson to wrench his reptile around, for already Alden and the Atlantean cavalrymen were speeding across the wide paved court, their lance pennons fluttering bravely in the orange-hued glare.

At top speed the rescuers dashed for a great, oval gateway while the podokos increased their gait; like aeroplanes gathering speed, the faster the weird creatures traveled, the higher arose their tails.

Then, following the frightened, backward glances of the hard-riding, red-haired lancers, Nelson suddenly discovered a new and terrible cause for this headlong flight, for, issuing from an unbarred gateway, came perhaps a dozen of *the terrible and enormous allosauri*, which, spying the fleeing cavalry, instantly gave chase.

With a sense of despair, the aviators heard the ferocious bellows booming from behind and watched the appallingly swift progress of those uncouth monsters as, leaping high into the air, the allosauri covered between fifty and sixty feet at a single bound.

"They'll get you," cried an inner voice in Nelson's being. "They'll catch you sure." But the small and lithe podokos, sensing death leaping up from the rear, stretched out their slender, snake-like heads, stood on tiptoe, and, pressing their small forelegs tight against their chests, commenced to run far faster than any horse could gallop. Nevertheless, the allosauri came bounding up like colossal kangaroos, uttering weird, screaming roars that brought a chill of imminent death to the fugitives.

Casting a quick glance over his shoulder, Nelson's blood froze to find an allosaurus not more than seventy yards behind, and making terrible exertions to close that slender gap! Nearer and nearer coursed the incredible monster, body rocking in its terrific stride, dreadful jaws wide apart—jaws that could, without an effort, cut a horse in half.

A fear such as he had never known racked Nelson's consciousness as he found he was hindermost of the cavalcade, which was strung out like a field of racers. The other riders crouched low in their saddles like jockeys, lances held straight out before them, and furiously goaded their strange mounts with curious hooks. Nelson was vastly relieved to get a glimpse of Alden far in the lead, almost beside the Atlantean Prince. His podoko was evidently better than the average.

Faster and faster pursuers and pursued raced across level meadows, over straight, white roads and rolling grain fields. Wind whistled madly in Nelson's ears, filled his eyes with tears, and made his short, dark hair snap, but two huge allosauri were now not twenty yards behind and *gaining with appalling speed!*

On the verge of madness, Nelson hammered his heels into the podoko's scaly side and wished he dared let go the saddle horn to draw his pistol, but to loose his grip was to risk falling off.

Closer and closer! Two enormous nightmarish heads were actually snapping at the fleeing podoko's tail. Then fear must have inspired the reptile Nelson bestrode, for it put on a sudden desperate burst of speed which carried it past the next two lancers. In passing he glimpsed the doomed wretches, pale-faced and horrified, as they frantically goaded their failing podokos.

A moment later, piercing screams from just behind assailed Nelson's ears, but when he looked to the rear once more it was to find that a wide gap had opened between him and the great monsters behind. Evidently, the heavy-built allosauri were unable to long maintain the terrific pace set by the smaller and more agile podokos whose maximum speed Nelson judged to be well over sixty miles an hour.

The pilot's eyes narrowed on beholding, in clear relief and not far away, the majestic, whitish outline of mighty Heliopolis, whose lofty towers, graceful domes and frowning citadels shone pink under the leaping, blinding glare on Mount Pelion.

"We certainly picked a nice time to drop in on this God-forsaken country," grunted Alden as the walls of Heliopolis loomed near. "We seem to have crashed into the busiest days they've had in centuries. How many shots you got?"

Nelson, swaying to the steady trot of his podoko, hesitated.

"Only five. Damned if I know what's going to happen next. I suppose it all depends on Hero Giles. Looks as though the nobles were bent on restoring Altorius—if he's not dead by now."

Alden tugged powerfully at the strange bridle which controlled his beast. "The priests wouldn't dare kill him, but it surely looks like their rebellion has gained a lot of headway."

A moment Alden's clear, blue eyes swept the towering battlements, gorgeously-sculptured temples and curious stepped pyramids, which now loomed near at hand and cast their rugged outlines sharp against the copper-colored heavens.

"Maybe there's some way we can work this revolution trouble to help us," suggested Nelson, without enthusiasm. "If we could play off one crowd against the other—"

His remarks were cut short as the foremost lancers slowed before an enormous bronze gate looming ahead. On the vast main panel was a beautifully-wrought dolphin curling about a trident—symbol of the imperial power now so sorely tried. Beyond that gate, breathlessly mused Nelson, lay Heliopolis and an unknown fate.

CHAPTER IX

It would have taken no trained eye to observe that something very unusual had happened in Atlans. Some of Heliopolis' many wide streets were quite desertsssed save for several small, bright-red cat-like reptiles that the Atlanteans sheltered as pets, but in other thoroughfares large throngs of people milled uneasily about, while listening to the impassioned harangue of black-robed priests. Everywhere business was at a standstill, shops were closed and markets tenantless.

Riding at an easy hopping gallop, the aviators urged their green, scaly mounts to the side of Hero Giles, for here and there some wandering citizens, spying the Americans, would yell shrill curses and shake their fists. Reining in, Nelson demanded to know the reason for this unaccountable hostility.

"'Tis the work of our gentle and holy priests," explained Hero Giles with a hard laugh. "They have told the populace ye are magicians seeking to set other gods above Poseidon."

"Nonsense," rapped the American, looking about uneasily. "We've never given two thin damns about anything except getting back to our plane."

"So I know," was the Atlantean's preoccupied reply; "but this spawn of Herakles' temples speak loud, and the loutish populace hearkens to their lies!"

"But what the devil is all this revolt about?" broke in Alden. "Why were we arrested? You started to tell us at the prison."

Hero Giles frowned as he pulled his podoko into a gracefully carved gateway of green marble. "There's but little to add, for 'tis all very simple. The priests have laid impious hands on His Splendor, Altorius, and imprisoned him in the great temple of Poseidon. We nobles have defied the arch-priest, for the dog-conceived Jereboam already marshals his forces for a fresh attack, knowing that Atlans is sore beset by internal strife. Have patience for now we go to the council chamber, where ye shall hear everything."

To say that the newcomers found the council of nobles in a furore would be to put it mildly. Their angry voices carried far down the beautifully ornamented corridors of the Imperial Palace, which was used as headquarters.

"Sounds like a dog-fight going on in there," muttered Alden anxiously. "Don't like the sound of it a bit. I hope they feel kindly towards us."

Nelson, swinging along with his ragged shirt fluttering like a scarecrow's, nodded. "Yes, so do I. But I guess they need our help or Hero Giles wouldn't have risked his life to save us."

Conscious of the value of appearances, the dark-haired aviator unconsciously straightened his frayed black tie, buttoned the sleeves of his khaki flannel shirt and other-wise made pathetic attempts at improving his appearance as the clamor of wrangling voices grew loud down the corridor.

His wide shoulders swinging to his stride, Hero Giles flung open a door, beautifully wrought with leaping podokos, and halted on the threshold.

"Death!" rumbled a voice from inside. "I say death to the Wanderers! Let us make our peace with the priests, lest they slay His Splendor forthwith."

"And that's what I call a nice friendly greeting," was Alden's murmured comment. "Better get your gat handy, Vic. I'll bet they've got a reception committee of retortii men behind the door."

There was no time for Nelson to reply because now the threshold was at hand. Inside, seated at a table, he had an impression of perhaps ten or fifteen scarred and angry-looking veteran nobles whose green cloaks and bejeweled armor revealed their high rank.

In mid-dispute they halted, eyeing the three figures in the doorway with curiously conflicting expressions. Some smiled a relieved welcome, some stared in surprise, but not a few greeted the Americans with lowering brows and angry, threatening eyes.

"Harken," Hero Giles greeted them. "By Poseidon's grace the Wanderers were saved from a vile death. Rise Heroes, and bid them welcome!"

"Ah, the Wanderers!" In an instant Hero John was wringing Nelson's hand. "Oh blessed hour! I had feared for ye both. Welcome, Hero Alden!"

A faint flush crept over the young man's wan and trouble-lined face. "'Tis well ye've come," he whispered. "The council was prepared to change their intent towards ye."

A grizzled, one-eyed prince arose, and leveling an accusing forefinger at Nelson shouted, "'Tis he hath caused the rebellion. Slay him!"

"Nay!" thundered the Hero Giles, "and forget not, Hero Paul—*I* am senior Prince of Atlans!"

In the great white marble council chamber silence fell, while from wonderfully carved ivory and gold chairs the harassed, yellow-bearded princes regarded the two uneasy Americans.

"Hearken, Hero Giles!" rasped another dark-browed officer in a plain, much-dented red breast plate. "I side with Paul. Away with them, I say! Time is too precious. Do not the dark hordes of Jereboam beat back our frontiers?"

Hero Giles glowered and sat bolt upright in his chair—a

strange disordered figure among his gorgeously robed and armored peers. "Thou wert ever a hothead! I prithee pause a moment! Remember how the dark-haired Wanderer once aided our imprisoned Emperor, whom Poseidon protect! Perchance, Hero Nelson and his friend once more can aid us in this, our hour of need."

Map of Jarmuth and Atlans

A chorus of variously opined voices broke out, while Nelson with an eye to possible violence stood ready.

"Silence! Sirrah!" The fierce old veteran banged a powerful fist on a golden dolphin head forming his chair arm. "This idle wrangling accomplishes naught, and a thousand weighty matters await our attention. Is it true the phalanxes at Tricca have risen for the priests?"

Before Hero Giles could reply, a stalwart guard at the door flung it open to admit a dust and sweat-bathed courier who, darting forward, flung himself at Hero Giles' no less dusty feet. While the yellow-haired Prince started back muttering in amazement, the runner raised a shaking hand.

"Woe, woe to Atlans!" he panted. "Jarmuthian retortii men have crossed the boiling river. Cierum is fallen! Its garrison is drenched in clouds of fungus gas. But a handful escaped!"

"Speak on: is that all?" A terribly intent expression crept over the aquiline faces around the council table.

"Nay, spare thy servant!" begged the green kilted courier, raising sweaty, imploring hands. "I—I dare not—"

"Speak!" snarled Hero Giles, his blue eyes terribly lit. "Speak!—else thy carcass shall be flung to the pteranodons."

Wild-eyed, the fellow blinked fearfully about. The grim-lipped nobles edged closer. Nelson, realizing all that lay at stake, watched intently, conscious that Alden was now by his side.

"I—I, Her Sacred Holiness, Altara—." The messenger's red face twitched and he choked as in terror.

"Altara!" The name reechoed weirdly from a dozen dry throats, and Nelson saw the skin suddenly pale and tighten over Hero John's face.

"What of the divine Altara, fool?" he thundered in a dreadful, shaken monotone. "Have those foul swine of Jarmuth dared—?"

"Forgive, oh Hero!" cried the groveling courier, his long red hair sweeping the marble floor. "The dog-sired Jereboam hath made proclamation in Jezreel that the Sacred Virgin is doomed to perish on the altar of Beelzebub, their demon god, in two days' time!"

"What?" The great marble-walled chamber was shaken by an unearthly outcry as horror and rage struggled for mastery in the circle of tense faces surrounding the momentarily forgotten aviators.

Bedlam broke loose, while Hero Giles sat as though stunned, staring on the shivering runner at his feet.

Nelson, very much on the alert, could see that the announcement of Altara's impending death had produced nothing short of a cataclysm in the plans of the council.

Like men paralyzed by electric shocks, the yellow bearded veterans and nobles sat stupefied, frozen in their last gesture. Then, in the midst of their silent despair, came the sound of a curious, high-pitched horn that had in its note something of the eery wail of a fire siren. The effect was magical, for the nobles sprang up, hands on sword hilts and eyes searching the corridor.

"The priests!" gasped a short, broad-shouldered noble at Altorius' left. "By Poseidon! 'Tis the fanfare of the Herakles himself."

Then indeed did the council glower, for, as Nelson soon learned, Herakles was the moving spirit and evil genius of that priestly party which had dared to imprison the Emperor.

Again the horn wailed its warning of the arch-priest's approach, whereat a stalwart hoplite in green painted armor clanked in, saluted stiffly and waited for Hero Giles' instructions.

"Bid the old man enter," directed the Prince at last. "Tell the graybeard he has naught to fear if he comes alone. Otherwise, bid him return to his kennel in the temples."

A moment after the hoplite had vanished, there appeared in the doorway a tall, emaciated old man on whose silvery head was set a curious golden mitre ending in the shape of a wondrously bejewelled trident. The curious Americans noted that the arch-priest's robes were as black as his evilly glittering eyes, and were embroidered with curious cabalistic symbols done in silver thread. In his withered hand Herakles carried a ceremonial trident—the mark of the Head Priest of Poseidon.

As though wary of advancing, the arch priest paused in the doorway, not three feet from where Nelson stood poised for action.

All at once the gaunt figure in black raised thin hands to the dome far overhead and cried in high-pitched prophetic tones:

"Woe to Atlans! When perishes Altara, virgin of Poseidon the God-head, then shall a darkness fall on Atlans! Her cities shall be cast down, there will be a weeping and wailing in the land, for Beelzebub and his followers shall prevail! Woe to Atlans and woe to ye all, blasphemous nobles!"

Gripped by a superstitious awe, the generals and nobles fell into an uneasy silence, fearfully lowering their eyes and then glancing askance at the plain khaki clad figures standing alert in their corner.

Nelson, defiantly meeting their eyes, beheld Hero Giles staring fixedly before him, his powerful shoulders bowed as though bearing an overwhelming burden.

Deeper grew the silence of disaster while the American furiously searched his mind for some means of thwarting the death in store for him and his companion. By chance, a word of Hero Giles recurred, the "pteranodons." What in the devil was a pteranodon? He turned sidewise to Alden who stood, hands in the pocket of his leather jacket, also thinking deeply.

"Dick," he whispered. "You studied paleontology at college. Do you remember what a pteranodon was?"

"A what?" The younger aviator seemed to make a definite effort to return to the present. "A pteranodon? I'm not sure, Vic, but I think it was a kind of flying reptile related to the pterodactyl group."

He could go on no further, for Herakles, the arch-priest, raised his snowy head suddenly, his eyes blazing. "To save Atlans in her hour of trial, we demand that ye deliver to us the Wanderers. They shall die as an offering to Ares, God of War. Perchance he will preserve us." The arch-priest's deep-set and glittering eyes swept with venomous hatred the two calm-featured aviators, who looked very plain and unromantic in their flying jackets and khaki serge. "We, familiars of the Gods, herewith demand that the blasphemers perish on the War God's altar! Else shall ye all die unbeloved of the Gods!"

"And we do your bidding, will ye give us back His Splendor?" demanded Hero Giles.

"Nay—we priests do not bargain like hucksters."

Risking all, Nelson muttered a swift aside to Alden. "How big were those pteranodons?"

"Some species had a wing spread of twenty-five feet."

The muscular pilot's mouth closed into a firm, colorless line as he nodded and glanced at the vindictive old man who was by now white with fury.

Up sprang a good three-quarters of the nobles present and turned on the grim figure at the head of the board.

"Surrender the Wanderers!" they shouted. "We demand it!"

In another instant the death sentence would have been forced on Hero Giles, but Victor Nelson leaped forward, pistol menacing the raging gray-bearded priest.

"Listen, all of you!" he shouted in deep tones that were strangely authoritative. "Beware, foolish Princes, how you threaten us. Great is our knowledge and power: you've seen that already. Even now, the other Wanderer and I can save or ruin Atlans, as we wish! Have ye forgotten the battle by Lake Copias?"

The Princes, furious at the American's defiance, half rose, hand on sword hilt, but sank back at a swift, menacing gesture from Nelson's pistol.

"What sayest thou, mad fellow?" screeched the arch-priest, his black eyes bright as knife points. "Save Atlans—?" Fierce questioning was in his sombre, sunken eyes.

"I said," repeated Nelson, "that, if we choose, we can yet save your Altara and the Emperor from death."

"Impossible! He is mad!" shouted Paul, the one-eyed Hero. "Not the Gods themselves could rescue Altara from the claws of the demon Beelzebub!" The nearest nobles flung themselves back in their chairs and snarled threats of all kinds as they gripped their sword hilts.

Sensing an inescapable climax, the khaki-clad American raised his pistol, covering Hero Paul, the speaker. "Silence!" he rasped. "You're a thick-headed idiot not to see the truth. Can this priest save Altara? No! You know damned well he can't! And yet you'd have us killed."

"Now, Herakles," he swung on the priest, "about this Altara matter—if you'll restore Altorius unharmed, guarantee our safety, and punish those liars who condemned us to death, the other Wanderer and I will undertake to not only prevent the sacrifice of Altara, but to bring the Princess back as well!"

To all this Alden listened with increasing and indescribable dismay, his blue eyes round as marbles. "My God!" he whispered in an undertone. "What in the devil is Vic doing? *Undertake* is *right*, the crazy fool!"

"How will ye accomplish this mad boast?" demanded the arch-priest in deep suspicion. "Know ye that the Sacred Virgin lies captive in the dungeons of the great temple of Beelzebub? Know ye that this temple is in the center of Jezreel, capitol of Jarmuth?"

"I had some idea that was the case."

"Know ye," continued, the graybeard priest, "that Altara is ever guarded by two thousand picked priests and warriors? Know ye, moreover, that this vile sacrifice will be made but two days hence?"

The aviator's lean, dark head inclined with a serenity he far from felt.

At this point the scarred veteran officer who had spoken before broke in, his face menacing. "Believe not this liar, oh Hero Giles! He speaks with a tongue made bold by fear. He promises that which he cannot accomplish!"

Had Victor Nelson had time to reflect upon the weirdness of the plan he had evolved, he would probably have silently admitted that his grizzled accuser was more than a little justified, but as it was he smiled serenely.

From all sides rose a threatening shout. "Let the blasphemers be sacrificed. Ares will protect us!"

His yellow brows knit, Hero Giles wavered, but as he hesitated there ran through a great circular window a distant yet menacing shout. "Down with Altorius, the Unlucky! Down with the sons of Hudson! Give back to the ancient Gods their Sacred Virgin. Hail to Ares! Death to the Wanderers! Death! Death!"

Drowning out these ominous cries there came from below the window the brazen clang of trumpets and the clank of many armored men hurrying forward. Presently the mob's outcry grew fainter, but still the cries of "Death" could be heard.

It was a tense moment. Would Hero Giles remain friendly? With poignant anxiety, Nelson watched that dishevelled martial head sink forward in perplexity.

"Hero Giles," he warned, in a low voice. "You'd better trust us. You're risking nothing."

Slowly, the fierce blue eyes of the veteran rose, and, meeting the level gray ones of the aviator, lingered there as though asking a question. Suddenly reaching a determination, he rose to his feet and addressed the triumphantly grinning arch-priest, who tightly clutched his trident wand with thin, blue-veined fingers.

"Hearken, black crow of a priest, who has dared lay foul hands on His Splendor, the Emperor. This is my reply: show me how ye will rescue Altara; otherwise begone! My hand itches for the sword."

A deep silence fell while Herakles glowered helplessly, then shrewdly avoided the trap. "This is blasphemy!" he croaked and raised a quivering forefinger in solemn warning. "Woe to thee, Hero Giles. Woe to the people! Fear the wrath of the Gods!

"Jeer not, ye nobles!" Herakles stormed on. "Be not deceived by lies! I bid thee deliver these magicians to Ares, God of War!"

A nasty moment; Nelson's heart drummed as he gazed down at the row of uneasy, war-like faces, but Hero Giles proved the strength of his heritage. Back went his patrician head; he drew himself up to full height and stared coldly upon the black robed priest, who, nothing daunted, gave back look for look.

"Nay! We keep them: they will bear out their promise. I give ye good day, oh Holiness!"

Quivering with rage Herakles raised his withered hand in anathema. "Then perish, blind spawn of Hudson! Verily shall ye all die under the torture. Woe! Woe! Woe!"

Then, amid a strained silence, pregnant of distrust and disaster, the old man wheeled and stalked out.

As he watched the departure, color drained from the Atlantean prince's haggard features. "Ah," he observed bitterly, "ever have these black crows feasted on our land,

and ever as birds of ill omen." He turned and, with a weary sigh, surveyed the group of loyal, but anxious souls. "I thank ye. Will ye still do my bidding and help to save our sovereign lord?"

Out flashed the swords of a dozen-odd nobles as they raised the hoarse, ringing cry of "Altorius! Altorius! Supreme!"

A little later Nelson, before a very mistrustful gathering composed of Hero Giles, Hero John and two or three other veterans, traced the barest outline of his plan.

"You understand? I'm to be taken to the border as a prisoner; then, in plain sight of the enemy lines, the guards must maltreat me and turn me loose."

The aviator searched one after another of the brutal, war-like faces, while Hero Giles translated for the benefit of two Atlantean generals who did not speak the royal language.

"Are you positive," Alden demanded of Hero John, "that this revolution in Atlans will die out if Altara is returned?"

"Yes! A thousand times yes!" The prince's fine eyes gleamed with savage enthusiasm. "With the Sacred Virgin restored to Atlans, new courage will come into the phalanxes! The priests will cease their outcries against them. Then, with the help of the blue maxima vapor, we will rend the dog-begotten followers of Jereboam limb from limb!"

"All right." Nelson's wiry khaki-clad body bent far over the table. "Remember, Hero Giles, that part of the fighting's up to you. When I'm gone, you'll do exactly what Alden tells you. Now, one thing more: what part of the border is still unquestionably loyal?"

Hero Giles frowned and shrugged his armor-clad shoulders a little helplessly beneath the splendid cloak of imperial green. "The gods alone know; but at the third division of this morning, Mayda and Thebes still vowed their loyalty. 'Tis there are quartered the phalanxes of the Imperial guards. They alone can I trust to the death."

"All right." Bending over a huge parchment map of the valley, Nelson nodded, and his keen black eyes became very serious. "I want you to concentrate every man you can muster in each of those cities. Meanwhile tell the populace,"—he drew a deep breath—"that Altara will certainly be returned to them."

"Art thou sure?" broke in the scarred veteran in the dented breast plate; then, his brow dark with doubt, he engaged Hero Giles and the rest in a heated, low-voiced colloquy.

Alden stepped near, an anxious frown on his unshaven features. "Think this idea of yours is sure-fire?"

"No," Nelson's lean head shook. "I'm far from sure. It's a wild gamble at best, but we can't be any worse off than we are now. If the priests win out, we're sunk and no mistake about it; but there's a fighting chance my idea could be brought off."

"Now look here," objected the younger pilot tensely. "What's this rot about your going into Jarmuth alone? How d'you know they won't skin you alive once you're over the border?"

"I don't," admitted his friend, shrugging slightly. "But I don't see there's anything but to take the risk. If I don't go over there, sure as shooting we're going to feed some damn unpleasant kind of beast here in Atlans.

"Another thing," Nelson said, turning to the Hero who, surrounded by the others, was bent in deep consultation over a map. "How am I to know Altara if I see her? Is there a statue, a painting or something—?"

The Hero's aquiline features lit in a slow smile. "Nay, we have better than that. Come, thou shalt see the Sacred Virgin as she now is."

The members of the conference followed Hero Giles down a short corridor, through a couple of doors and into a chamber where a huge disc of crystal stood on edge fixed upon an axis above a bewildering array of wires, pipes and gauges.

Hero John, who seemed familiar with the mechanism, turned a lever, whereupon the disc commenced to spin like a pie plate on a dance floor. Faster and faster it spun, silently gathering speed each second while a low humming sound filled the chamber. Gradually the outline of the whirling disk commenced to brighten, tinting the scar-seamed, craggy features of the Atlantean generals and picking glorious, glowing lights from the jewels on Hero Giles' wonderfully engraved breastplate.

"Ah." Hero John turned a small dial. "The crystal warms. Look, oh Wanderers!"

Nelson rubbed his eyes incredulously, for in the heart of the shimmering circle had materialized the outline of a room with walls of yellow marble.

"Well, I'm damned!" gasped Alden. "See how it flickers!"

As the revolving disc of crystal gained top speed, the flickering subsided and a picture, clearer than most photographs, could be seen in the center. A wondrously slender, yellow-haired young girl clad in Grecian robes of pale blue sat in deep despond upon a plain wooden couch, with a black haired servant kneeling before her, apparently lacing sandals on her tiny, pink-hued feet.

"Bring closer the face," snapped Hero Giles gruffly.

Gradually the focus changed, like the close-up of a movie camera, until in the center of the madly whirling disc could be seen in minute detail and living color the face of an indescribably lovely girl.

"Whew," muttered Nelson, staring in silent amazement. "No wonder they want her back! She makes Ziegfeld's little girls look like Armenian refugees." He cast a side-wise glance, but Alden had apparently not heard him; the younger American stood gazing with rapturous joy at the girl.

"Aye! Aye!" The two veteran generals uttered stifled groans and one of them drew a hand across his eyes. "Poseidon save her! Aye! Preserve the fair Altara."

"Wouldst thou not doubly save her, now?" demanded Hero John in a low voice that bespoke his anguish. He seemed suddenly older than the grim, helmeted veterans to either side.

"You bet! I guess a man sees a face like that only once is a lifetime. And now," Nelson continued with an effort to return to the practical, "there's no time to be lost—so I'd just like to take a look at those pteranodons of yours."

A few minutes later, the two aviators found themselves nearing a lofty structure which adjoined the imperial palace. It was constructed along the lines of an immense aviary. Between beautiful, glistening Ionic columns of white marble, gleamed bronze bars, set at regular intervals to prevent the escape of the most appalling creatures which could ever have skimmed the air.

"What in the devil is your idea?" demanded Alden, taken aback. "God, look at the loathsome brutes!"

Some of these huge, flying reptiles were hopping

awkwardly over the ground picking at bones and refuse littering the floor with long pelican-like bills, which were, however, very much thicker than those of pelicans, and set with sharp teeth at least six inches long.

"Not very pretty are they? Kind of look like huge bats," commented Nelson thoughtfully. "Wonder if they could be handled?"

"Yes, their wings are leathery. Look at 'em up yonder." Alden pointed to the roof of that immense aviary where, hanging head downwards like gigantic bats, must have been hundreds upon hundreds of the pteranodons. One of them, whistling oddly, fluttered up to the bars, affording the Wanderers an excellent view of a loathsome head, the back of which ended in a curious sort of horn, that, projecting backwards, jutted far above its rear. Fierce, vermillion eyes with green irises glared at the Americans through the bars, and great wings of greasy-looking leather fanned a disgusting stench from the interior of the aviary.

"Sweet little things," was Alden's comment. "God! Imagine having one of those great things swooping down on you. Hey, Alden, look at that big devil over there! He must have a wing spread of thirty feet. Big as a Moth plane, isn't he?"

For answer the pteranodon clattered its vast beak savagely. One of the generals stooped and, catching up a huge slab of meat from a basket nearby, hurled it through the bars into the gaping jaws.

"What would ye with these creature?" demanded Hero Giles with undisguised curiosity.

"You'd be surprised." Nelson was not deliberately rude, but his mind was wrapped up in the daring project he had evolved. "I want a couple of the biggest of these caught and set aside in a courtyard where there will be no one looking on. If your people can train and handle podokos and allosauri—I guess a couple of Yanks ought to be able to manage these flying nightmares. So don't you worry about us."

Hero Giles uttered grim, significant laugh. "Thou hadst best manage them. I note yonder pteranodon is in need of nourishment."

CHAPTER X

With sharp anxiety, Victor Nelson kept watching the towers of Jezreel rise ever clearer above the great, warm plain of Jarmuth, but, for all that, he noted how distinctly Jezreel differed from Heliopolis. The Jarmuthian capital was predominantly amber-yellow instead of white in color; its towers were flat-topped, angular, hideous structures that compared not at all favorably with the graceful Grecian architecture of Atlantean public buildings.

The populace, he decided, as he strode along in the midst of half a dozen silent guards, were as harsh and graceless as their architecture. Whereas the Atlanteans had been white skinned and uniformly red haired—save for those of Hudsonian blood—the inhabitants of Jarmuth almost without exception were black haired and had dark, olive-hued skins.

"They're the lost tribes of Israel, all right," Nelson decided after a brief sojourn in that savage land lying beyond Apidanus—the great boiling river, whose bubbling and scalding currents had for centuries served as a natural boundary between the two realms. But now the Jarmuthian armies had crossed it and were steadily pushing back the demoralized and despairing Atlanteans with savage energy that heaped the dead in hillocks.

"Their armor," mused the ragged, barefoot prisoner, studying his silent guards, "looks a lot like a Roman legionnaire's, but that six pointed star on their helmets is pure Semitic. Yes, this sure is an Asiatic outfit."

His eyes wandered from one fierce, big-nosed infantryman to another and noted the splendid physical structure of the majority. Evidently hardier, much less refined and luxury-loving than the Atlanteans, these swart warriors disdained robes and other garments. Save for helmet, armor and brief black kilts, they were quite naked. Like the Atlantean hoplites the infantrymen carried spears, steam retortii and quantities of grenades.

The country side through which the prisoner passed had a holiday air, for garlands of flowers hung in every doorway, and naked, pot-bellied children squatted by the roadside, industriously weaving crowns and streamers of gay blossoms.

"Look, Atlantean dog!" commanded the black-bearded leader of the escort. "Let thine infidel eyes gaze upon the mightiest city of the world. Seest thou yonder Ziggurat which o'er towers all others?"

Nelson raised eyes red-rimmed from sleeplessness and deep anxiety—for the crafty Jarmuthians had proved unexpectedly unwilling to credit him as the Atlantean outcast and would-be renegade he had pretended to be.

"Yes," he said in reply to the English-speaking *jehar's*—captain's—question. "What's it for?"

"'Tis the temple of the almighty Beelzebub, Steam God of Jarmuth. Without his hot breath no wheel would turn, our armies would be powerless and this land would perish under the ice of the outer world." The dark eyed officer's eye fell speculatively upon his bound and dust-covered prisoner. "Perchance, dog of a spy, thou wilt die during today's fourth division[2] together with Altara, pale daughter of the feeble, false god Poseidon."

his afternoon?

Nelson could not realize that the time had flown so quickly. Four short hours separated him from the crisis of

2   The Atlantean day was divided into six divisions of four hours each; due to the flame suns there was no sunrise or sunset.

his life. A thousand doubts assailed him. What if Alden or Hero Giles failed in their share of the great scheme for rescue? Narrowly, the aviator's eye searched the great, rich plain, then swept the amber-hued sky where, far above the plain, Jilboa, the nearest flame sun, beat off the Arctic chill and darkness.

The great, black-bearded jehar eased the straps from which was suspended the brass coil of his retortii. "Aye," he chuckled, his thick lips parted in a crafty smile. "Ere long will the fair flesh of Altara grace the ceremonial board of His Exaltation, the King, and his priests and princes."

Nelson gasped in horror. The divinely beautiful Altara— butchered for meat like a calf? Grotesque! Ghastly! "What! You eat your prisoners?" He felt sick, nauseated.

For answer, the swart Jarmuthian raised an enormous hand and dealt the captive American a stinging cuff which made his teeth rattle.

"Peace!" he snarled. "Else I slit thy spying throat ere we pass yonder walls."

Fingering a short blue-black beard that was frizzed into tight curls in the Assyrian manner, the jehar lengthened his stride as the little detachment clanked into the shadow of a great wall surrounding Jezreel, and through a huge gate guarded by two hideous, jackal-headed effigies.

Hurrying into the city were throngs of eager men, women and children, interspersed with muscular, black bearded soldiers who cast threatening, baleful eyes on the pale-skinned prisoner.

At first the great metropolis of Jezreel seemed boundless, for everywhere arose tall, massive monuments of yellow marble whose facades were engraved with Sanskrit characters, thus bearing out Nelson's surmise that this was indeed a race of Semitic origin.

Here and there hurried grey-bearded, vulture-eyed priests oddly garbed in corrupt Occhive and Tyrian regalia. Nelson found it odd to see the Tablet of the Laws, which Jarmuth so openly ignored, swaying on their yellow robed breasts; and none cried out more menacingly nor more loudly against the limping, wan-faced captive, than these same ecclesiastics, who must have long since forgotten all worship of Jehovah in the foul service of a bestial golden effigy.

A stone sailed through the air, narrowly missing the American; then another, which struck his shoulder.

"God, what a rough looking crowd," thought Nelson, as the guards, cursing, held back the screaming mob. "At this rate I won't live to even reach the temple!"

Every second his life stood in great danger. Unkempt, sloe-eyed women hurled themselves, shrieking with fury, against the armored chests of the guards, who were hard pressed to beat them off with their spear hafts.

Nelson's one small ray of comfort in this evil hour was the fact that his .45 pistol remained untouched in a food wallet. At the border the jehar had cast one contemptuous glance at the weapon, but, no doubt deeming it some strange culinary tool, he had made no effort to remove it.

It was a continual struggle for the guards to win their way up a long flight of stairs, for ever the great stream of humanity grew denser and more menacing.

Nelson felt a violent sense of revolt grip his being. "I must win free," he thought. "If I fail, Alden dies, and—and—" For the first time he realised how much he wanted to actually see Altara. Like a clear cameo, an image of her had remained fresh in his memory. Except for her Grecian garments she might have been a lovely, carefree English or American girl.

"And these decadent swine would sacrifice her!" The thought was sickening. Yet how could he prevent the pitiful tragedy?

Fortunately, a detachment of troops—tall, sinewy fellows with conical helmets, crested with six-pointed stars—reenforced the guards just as clawing hands began to snatch and tug at the prisoner's ragged Atlantean chiton of blue cotton.

Almost before he realized it, Nelson was dragged inside a great gloomy building and into a circular chamber where four eagle-featured elders sat in council beneath the six-pointed star of Sem. On approaching, the jehar in command sank on one knee and in humble salute raised both hands to the tribunal.

"A tough looking desk sergeant they've got," muttered the prisoner to himself as his eye met the chilling regard of a lean, yellow-faced priest. "Wonder what I'm booked for?" Idiotically, he recalled being summoned before a traffic court, years back. "Guess I don't get off with vagrancy; it'll probably be everything from speeding to mayhem, with maybe arson and well-poisoning thrown in."

The deliberations of this ominous court proved to be appallingly short. The dour-faced elders merely put their heads together, muttered a few sentences, then straightened up almost immediately. The chief priest—he with the yellow face—thrust out his fist and made the immemorial signal of death by jerking his thumb at the black marble floor.

Before the outraged and astounded aviator could utter

a word of protest, powerful guards seized and hauled him off down a dark, narrow passageway in which the fetid prison smell was very strong. Too wise to struggle against overwhelming odds, yet appalled at the thought of his impending doom, Nelson was dragged into a room where four or five furtive, enslaved Atlanteans, made dumb by the removal of their tongues, were engaged in a curious occupation.

On a bare stone bench, five other Atlantean captives were sitting in miserable silence. They made a grotesque array, for their heads were crowned with gay yellow and blue flowers, and the upper half of their perfectly formed bodies gleamed with an application of a sweet-smelling oil. About their wrists and waists were twined fragrant garlands of yellow roses which hid the leather straps confining their hands.

Struggling, Nelson was forced on to the bench, whereupon slaves, skipping to avoid the lash of a scarred, olive-hued slave driver, hurried to wash the newly arrived prisoner's limbs, face and hands. A weary-looking old slave with sunken, rheumy eyes listlessly pulled the blue chiton from Nelson's broad shoulders, and would have removed the food pouch had not the prisoner winked vigorously. The ministering slave glanced swiftly sidewise and, discovering the slave driver's attention directed to another corner, pulled the upper folds of the chiton over the food pouch and its precious contents, then set a crown of yellow roses more or less askew on the American's head. For all the peril of the situation Nelson could not suppress a fleeting smile as the phrase, "For I'm to be Queen of the May, Mother," leaped nonsensically into his brain.

"Yes, I guess they are getting us all dolled up for a sacrifice of some kind." Nelson's heart began to pound at the thought. Then he fought for self control. It must be a hideously realistic nightmare! He, Victor Nelson, American citizen, a quiet birdman, member of the Caterpillar Club and ex-flight commander of the A. E. F. was about to be offered as a sacrifice to some hideous, pagan god? Nonsense! He'd wake up in a minute and hear the drone of a ship on the line.

He blinked, staring fixedly at a single ray of light that came streaming in through a small, barred window, then glanced sidewise at his fellow victims, who with Spartan indifference sat waiting for the end of all things. It was no dream!

From the tiny window came the shrill discordant braying of many trumpets, and a roar like that of a football crowd arose surprisingly near. In response, the slave driver lashed the gaudily bedecked sacrificial victims to their feet with vicious cuts of his pliant whip, and herded them like a drove of calves down a very long passage, lit at intervals by those strange column lamps of incandescent gas. In their red glare the doomed six seemed as though already bathed in blood.

"Must be some crowd of people outside," muttered Nelson as a great gale of sound deafened him. Yonder the amber glare of the flame suns glimmered, and now it was his turn to step into the open!

On a sort of spiral roadway he paused, breathless, awed, bewildered, for there, eddying restlessly about the bases of towers and other huge structures, was a great sea of up-turned faces. To his surprise he found the passage he had followed opened perhaps halfway up what must be the great Ziggurat of Beelzebub. He judged the tower's height must be immense, for already the crowd was a good hundred feet below.

"*Zarotoa! Zarotoa! ù Wlanka!*"[3]

Nelson shivered. How terrible was the wild, bloodthirsty clamor of that vast throng, when they beheld the six flower-decked prisoners appear upon the circular winding road which led to the lofty and wind-swept summit of the great conical pyramid of the people of Jezreel.

Behind the victims marched perhaps eighteen or twenty spearmen gorgeously uniformed in yellow and black painted armor. Their retortii were plated with gold, and in the center of a star forming the crest of each helmet was set a diamond large as a hickory nut.

Preceding the despairing prisoners marched a squad of tall, clean-shaven priests with great gold hoops in their ears. They blew mightily upon long, curved horns, and were followed by perhaps a dozen lithe, posturing girls, half clothed in diaphanous yellow robes. These priestesses swung golden censers which flung bluish clouds of aromatic smoke high into the humid air above.

Up and up, around and around the great tower temple, Nelson was dragged, while the vast city of Jezreel, palaces, towers, courts, dwellings and all, lay like a great panorama below. Up and up, and the wind grew stronger while Nelson marvelled at the great height of the structure he was mounting. Immediately in front of him swayed the naked shoulders of the three captive Atlanteans; he could see rose petals from their crowns fluttering in the strong warm breeze sweeping that man-made pinnacle for the worship of a heathen god.

---

3   Death to the victims!

Despairingly, the American's eyes searched the horizon, to discover nothing but a few great birds wheeling lazily in the bronze-hued sky. Very clearly he could discern three of the flame suns, casting flame high from their peaks.

"Alden!" he groaned. "Oh God, Alden, don't fail me!"

Chilled by the fate in store, he scanned the dark and hostile faces below, but found no friendly visage.

Up and up. The procession was now nearing the summit.

There were hosts of poignant problems before him, each vital if Altara and the Empire of Atlans were to be saved; but one primary question immediately confronted him. How could he get his hands free? He ventured a few words in English to the stolid Atlantean at his side, whereat the fellow only stared dully and shook his red, flower-crowned head.

He next tried to cautiously work loose his hands, but to no avail. The rope of plaited skin binding his aching wrists together was tough as any rawhide. Cursing, he abandoned the effort, and, as his eyes once more swept the great blood-thirsty throng below, he felt himself doomed indeed.

CHAPTER XI

Standing at last on the summit of the great Ziggurat, Nelson found himself staring up at the fearsome golden image of the dread demon Beelzebub. The god stood some twelve feet in height and had a hideous human face, but, in place of hair and beard, countless golden tubes writhed in all directions. From the end of one, the puzzled prisoner beheld several tiny feathers of steam creeping forth, indicating that these hairs were a species of steam vent.

When, with the other captives, he was made to halt near its base, he further discovered that the idol sat upon a throne of yellow marble, the sides of which were carved with Sanskrit characters, necessarily quite meaningless to the doomed aviator.

In a grim and silent rank before Beelzebub's feet, stood some six or eight priest-executioners bending their black-robed bodies against the strong wind which swept that ghastly pinnacle.

Just below the base of the image, Nelson noted several great, copper coils, no doubt conducting steam from the interior of the Ziggurat. Between the knees of Beelzebub rested a huge, shallow bowl, the use of which puzzled the American not a little, for he saw that the base of this ornate receptacle was also wrapped with a number of steam coils. Two great hands, ending in cruel-looking claws, were stretched horizontally above the demon's knees, seeming to plead for victims.

Suddenly a deep toned brazen gong sounded somewhere below; the trumpeters blew an ear-piercing note; and, at a gesture from the high priest, four of the brawny executioner-priests leaped forward, seized one of the Atlantean victims, hurled him to the stone platform and, in an unbelievably short interval, strapped the shrieking wretch by wrists, elbows, knees and ankles to a long, brass rod. Slung like a dead deer from a rail, they lifted the helpless Atlantean, and, while five hundred thousand voices roared in acclaim the priests fitted the pole ends into notches above the hands of the idol with the effect that the idol actually seemed to be clutching its victim.

Then, from all the pipes composing the hair and beard of Beelzebub, sprang forth hissing spouts of snowy steam which, whipped by the rising wind, went whirling madly down the lee of the Ziggurat. At the same time, from the half open mouth of the demon issued a fearful, screaming howl, a thousand times louder than the whistle of a speeding locomotive. Deafening and barbaric, it was reechoed from a hundred towers and battlements.

A dreadful, exultant well burst from the multitude below as the red-robed priest drew from beneath his garments a sickle-shaped knife that glittered evilly in the light of the flaming suns. Still chanting, he stooped and quickly made a deep incision over the heart of the victim. While a piercing, agonized shriek burst from the ashen lips of the doomed Atlantean, his bright life-blood began to splash into the golden bowl below where, due to the presence of the steam coils, it swiftly commenced to hiss and bubble. Very quickly the last scarlet drops had fallen.

Then while Nelson, sick and horrified, stood watching, the dead body on its pole was taken down, unstrapped, and hurled, limp and red-spattered, to the next lower platform where other priests waited to dismember it for the ceremonial cannibalism soon to follow.

In rapid succession two more victims were slaughtered amid the blood-hungry cheers of the Jarmuthian populace.

Now the great bowl hissed and bubbled with a generous supply of the dark red fluid, from which rose clouds of evil-smelling steam that fanned the hideous features above.

From below suddenly arose an excited shout far mightier than any which had preceded it, when the executioners, sweating from their exertions, now turned and, spying Nelson, hurried forward. Coincidently, the American's bound hands disappeared beneath the chiton. Squaring his shoulders, he gripped the pistol, prepared to make a good end.

"They'll get me, but before I die I'll send at least two or three of these devils to hell," he thought. "Come on—"

But, for an inexplicable reason, the arch-priest beckoned back his satellites, while roar upon roar of terrific excitement swelled from the swarming mob below, and a shout which at last became distinguishable bid fair to split the heavens. "Altara! Altara! Altara!"

Slowly, the temporarily reprieved victim's muscles stiffened. He understood. The next victim was to be the fair Altara, sister of Altorius and Sacred Virgin of Atlans.

"Altara! Altara!" A rising hurricane of impassioned human voices thundered the name.

Suddenly, the desire to live burned doubly strong in the American's breast. He must somehow prevent this inhuman catastrophe. But how? How?

Stealing a quick glance over his shoulder, Nelson stifled a groan. The southern horizon remained clear, and put an end to hope. No help! He must fight it out to the end alone.

A rank of exultant, black-bearded priests now appeared at the head of the stairway, then a quartet of olive skinned, semi-naked priestesses joyfully clashing brass cymbals.

There came an interval—and Nelson's heart stood still as there appeared the lovely head and shoulders of her whom he had first seen in the heart of the revolving crystal. Even more fiercely, mad revolt at fate gripped him.

Through hot, strained eyes the American saw that the stately Altara was beautiful beyond all possible comparison, and that she seemed utterly unafraid in the hour of her dreadful death. The Atlantean maiden's large, clear blue eyes were fixed with calm resignation on the distant flame sun of Jilboa. On her curling golden hair had been set a circlet of ceremonial yellow roses, while her white, slender body was thinly covered with a scanty robe of yellow silk.

Slowly, and moving her small bare feet in a regal stride, Altara climbed the last few steps and stood straight and unafraid before the hideous demon god of Jarmuth.

Thousands of frantic inner voices assailed the aviator's consciousness. "Save her! You must save her! She's too young, too beautiful to die!"

Like a vast maelstrom of sound, so swelled the lustful cry of the dark multitude at the base of the Ziggurat, while the arch-priest chanted his litany in a sort of triumphant exultation. Then, all at once, one of the executioners roughly tripped the golden haired girl, sprawling her helpless on the bloody stones; and, before Nelson could quite realize it, the slender, silver hued form lay limp and helpless between Beelzebub's bloody claws.

Like a dynamo furiously gathering speed, so buzzed Nelson's brain. He was going to save her—if only for a brief interval! One man against a nation. Through a raging mist of fury he saw the red-robed priest raise his lean arms; then the American's bound hands darted beneath the blue chiton to reappear immediately. No one saw the pistol, for every eye was rivetted upon the gleaming, sickle-knife of the red priest. Like a voice from hell, that eery scream burst again from Beelzebub's throat as his priest stepped near, the knife raised.

Amid a deafening roar the sickle-knife flashed higher; but it never fell, for the red priest suddenly reeled, clutched his chest and, staring wildly, staggered sidewise, while the assembled priests stared thunderstruck. The deafening roar of Beelzebub, the clamor of horns and cymbals had drowned out the report. In superstitious awe the Jarmuthians leaped back, panic-stricken, from the convulsively writhing body of the red priest, which rolled crazily down the steps before the idol; but a high shout of terror rang out as he toppled off the summit and, like a discarded puppet, plunged down the precipitous side of the cone-like tower.

Again Nelson's pistol spat, and two of the executioners collapsed in kicking agony. Like an avenging fury, the American raged about the summit, the pistol in his bound bands dealing death right and left until panic seized the remaining priests, who, with one accord, abandoned their weapons to rush headlong down the dizzy, winding roadway. In a trice, none but Altara, Nelson, the two Atlanteans and the fallen priests remained on the summit.

It was the work of a moment for the Atlanteans to cast loose Nelson's bound wrists, and he theirs; time was precious, for, from below, a furious cohort of spearmen were charging up the stairs, their dark features terrible in their wrath.

"Only four more shots!" The sickening realization dashed into Nelson's brain. "That'll never stop them." Then in the midst of his despair he saw an answer. Stepping back he fired twice full into the great steam coil circling the base of the idol.

Spang! Spang! His bullets smacked through the copper coil to puncture neat, round holes. As he fervently hoped, jets of live steam rushed through these vents with terrible force and bathed the head of the stairs with a scalding, blinding vapor. Howling like mad beasts, the agonized Jarmuthian hoplites fell back, while overhead Beelzebub bellowed incessantly, shaking the sky with his hideous voice.

"That's better." But Nelson knew his triumph to be brief. *"Where in hell is Alden?"* he raged as with shaking hands be released the bewildered girl from the death bar after the two Atlanteans had lifted it and its fair burden from the claws of Beelzebub.

Picking up the swords and other weapons of the fallen priests the two Atlanteans uttered their deep-toned war cry of *Halor vàn!* and joyously prepared to die fighting, as furious roar on roar of wrath arose from the populace, infuriated at being cheated of their prey. But the black-armored temple guards dared not charge those twin steam jets barring their approach. Accordingly they tried other means.

Nelson's heart stopped as a small, dark object sailed up from below and clattered on the platform. It was a grenade. With the speed of thought, the American kicked it to the landing below, where it exploded, annihilating a detachment of Jarmuthians by drenching them with the terrible fungus gas. Heart bounding with savage joy, Nelson watched the deadly green fog leap from the broken grenade and of its own accord settle on the nearest soldiers. With the usual astonishing speed there formed on the stricken soldiery that poisonous yellow mould, whose fungus-like shoots sprouted through nostrils and mouths. On the dense crowd below the bomb's effect was appalling, and no more grenades were hurled....

During the respite Nelson's anguished eyes once more

swept the skies. He started. Was it true or was it a mirage? Far to the southward a small, black speck materialized in the orange-hued heavens. Good old Alden! Hope wavered in the American's breast. Could he and his two fellows beat off the infuriated Jarmuthians long enough? He doubted it.

A shower of spears sailed up, but because of the angle, their trajectory was too great, and like rays of death the lances flashed harmlessly overhead to plunge over the summit and wreak death among those on the other side.

Nearer and nearer came the black speck while from the populace a low shout of amazement arose. Coincidently Nelson's heart stopped; aghast, he saw that the steam was no longer hissing from the holes at the idol's feet! Evidently, the steam current had been shut off from below to allow the raging priests to lead their followers in a desperate charge up the stairs.

Marshalling an Atlantean to either side, Nelson sprang to the head of the stair and fired full in the face of gorgeously robed priests who staggered back screaming. But the others wavered only an instant.

"*Halor vàn!*" Both Atlanteans hurled spears retrieved from the abandoned weapons—and each struck down his man.

The American's eye flickered up. Yes, there came a strange, but welcome sight: a great creature with enormous, leathery pinions was circling down towards the tower top! A clashing of weapons brought Nelson's eyes earthwards. He joined in a furious melée at the stair top, like the Atlanteans, using a captured bronze sword. There came a deep groan as the right-hand Atlantean collapsed with a bloodied bronze spear point standing far out from between his naked shoulder blades.

A swooping shadow fell across the slowly advancing attackers. Beholding that awesome creature the Jarmuthians cowered, hesitated; then in headlong panic they darted below, uttering howls of fear and pursued by the surviving Atlantean, who, gone berserk, must have shortly paid for his folly.

The pteranodon was now quite recognizable, and seated on a double saddle was Alden, skillfully guiding the ungainly monster by means of a curious bridle, by shifting his weight and by pressing certain nerve centers between the great reptile's leathery shoulders.

Down, down circled Alden until the great wings skimmed just above Beelzebub's ugly golden head.

Her courage strained beyond endurance, Altara screamed shrilly in fear as Alden guided the huge reptile to the summit and forced it to light.

"Quick!" shouted Alden. "They're coming back up!"

"All right!" Catching up the fainting girl, Nelson hurdled two or three fallen bodies, and, while Alden showered fungus bombs upon the returning Jarmuthians, he laid his precious burden across the saddle and secured her with straps specially designed for the purpose.

"All right, Dick," he snapped. "Get going!"

"But you?" Alden's brown face was terribly intent.

"I'm not going! This creature could never carry the three of us. It can't, I tell you! Hurry, those devils are coming!"

Alden folded his arms. "If you don't go, I don't."

"All right then," snarled Nelson, vaulting into the saddle after casting loose the inert, yellow-robed girl. "Be a damned fool! We'll all die now."

* * * * *

It was a near thing, for the pteranodon, scenting the fresh blood, was very loath to obey its master, and scuffed awkwardly around the tower top two or three times, while Nelson, clutching Altara to him, expended his last shot in driving back the enemy.

At last, the pteranodon spread its huge brown pinions and took off. Then Nelson gasped in alarm, for, unaccustomed to the heavy weight it now bore, the pteranodon scaled earthwards with the speed of a meteor, wildly flapping its bat-like-wings. Down! Down! Nelson had an impression of people scattering like frightened ants.

Alden cursed, tugged furiously on the bridle, and set his weight back in the saddle, but to no avail. Down! Ever down! The pteranodon now struggled among the tall buildings.

A sickening sense of defeat gripped Nelson as a long jet of steam shot out from a huge brass retortii mounted on the roof of an arsenal. The scalding fingers of steam just missed its target, but fortunately served to sting the descending pteranodon. With a convulsive shudder and a whistling scream, the hideous reptile commenced to flap its gigantic wings faster, and, slowly but surely, began to rise over the yellow temples and towers of the barbarous city of Jezreel.

What followed is now a matter of Atlantean history. On its pages is set forth in full detail how the giant pteranodon barely crossed the boiling river to sink exhausted in the outskirts of Tricca.

There, also, is described the series of tremendous battles in which the Atlanteans, led by Altorius and inspired by the return of their Sacred Virgin, employed the terrible fungus gas to overwhelm the Jarmuthian invaders, driving them back with great slaughter to the steaming plains of their own land.

At even greater length is described the great triumph Altorius accorded the victorious aviators on the occasion of Victor Nelson's marriage to Altara.

"Doth it not seem strange," she whispered as they stood looking out over the great, sleeping city of Heliopolis, "that thou of the New World and I of the Lost World, should stand man and wife?"

The American's tanned face softened. "My darling," he whispered, "there are lots of strange things in the new Atlantis—but this isn't one of them."

www.ingramcontent.com/pod-product-compliance
Lightning Source LLC
Chambersburg PA
CBHW020145180626
46810CB00004B/1747